Bola  **fallen**
sho **to fire**

"Kill me _____ endure the pain."

"Where d_ _ __ _oss go?"

"I don't know. Help me."

"I can end the pain," the Executioner promised. He had done so many times, even for his enemies.

"Please," the fallen mercenary pleaded. "He's at Courchevel 1800, at the Everest."

The Executioner raised his Uzi, placed it close to the dying man's ear and fired two mercy rounds. He stared at the body, and the others strewed about the factory floor. Wasted lives.

He felt no sympathy for any of the dead. They received what they had intended to deliver—death.

MACK BOLAN ®

The Executioner

DON PENDLETON'S
THE EXECUTIONER®
JACKAL HUNT

A GOLD EAGLE BOOK FROM
WORLDWIDE.

TORONTO • NEW YORK • LONDON
AMSTERDAM • PARIS • SYDNEY • HAMBURG
STOCKHOLM • ATHENS • TOKYO • MILAN
MADRID • WARSAW • BUDAPEST • AUCKLAND

First edition April 1998
ISBN 0-373-64232-6

Special thanks and acknowledgment to
David North for his contribution to this work.

JACKAL HUNT

Power exercised with violence has seldom been of long
duration....

—Seneca
B.C. 3-65 A.D.

Violence begets violence, especially when the bottom
line sees powermongers willing to go to the max to
ensure their profits are maintained, regardless of the cost
in human lives. When they choose to go up against the
President of the United States they cross the line—and
enter *my* territory.

—Mack Bolan

THE
MACK BOLAN®
LEGEND

Nothing less than a war could have fashioned the destiny of the man called Mack Bolan. Bolan earned the Executioner title in the jungle hell of Vietnam.

But this soldier also wore another name—Sergeant Mercy. He was so tagged because of the compassion he showed to wounded comrades-in-arms and Vietnamese civilians.

Mack Bolan's second tour of duty ended prematurely when he was given emergency leave to return home and bury his family, victims of the Mob. Then he declared a one-man war against the Mafia.

He confronted the Families head-on from coast to coast, and soon a hope of victory began to appear. But Bolan had broken society's every rule. That same society started gunning for this elusive warrior—to no avail.

So Bolan was offered amnesty to work within the system against terrorism. This time, as an employee of Uncle Sam, Bolan became Colonel John Phoenix. With a command center at Stony Man Farm in Virginia, he and his new allies—Able Team and Phoenix Force—waged relentless war on a new adversary: the KGB.

But when his one true love, April Rose, died at the hands of the Soviet terror machine, Bolan severed all ties with Establishment authority.

Now, after a lengthy lone-wolf struggle and much soul-searching, the Executioner has agreed to enter an "arm's-length" alliance with his government once more, reserving the right to pursue personal missions in his Everlasting War.

Porto Santos, Beruba

Sitting on the edge of the roof, Mack Bolan, a.k.a. the Executioner, relaxed his grip on the Stoner SR-25 and let it rest on its tripod. He was glad that he had been able to bring the sniper's rifle into the country. It was the perfect weapon for his current needs.

The big American was in the capital city of the small Caribbean nation of Beruba to check out the tip Hal Brognola had gotten. A Bolivian drug cartel had financed an assassination attempt on the life of the newly elected president. The hit would go down during his inauguration.

Bolan's mission was to work with government troops to prevent the hit and to take out the gunman before he could accomplish his goal.

The Stoner SR-25 sniper rifle was ideal for the conditions he faced. It could throw up to twenty rounds of 168-grain, .308-caliber power at a target more than one thousand yards away. Traveling at 2200 feet per second, the hollowpoint loads could be placed within a two-inch circle.

The single-space trigger had a four-and-one-half-pound pull, making it easy to fire without jerking the rifle.

Bolan lifted the Zeiss 10×30 binoculars hanging from a strap around his neck and studied the large, open square below him.

RUDOLFO AMIREZ, deputy commander of the presidential guard, was kneeling beside Bolan. He kept looking at the tall, well-built man he had been introduced to by the new president's secretary as Mike Belasko. The American was impressive. His body didn't seem to contain an ounce of extra fat, and his diamond-hard gaze had no expression. If Belasko hadn't been sent to protect the newly elected head of state, Amirez would have picked him out as the most likely to be a professional assassin.

The deputy commander turned his attention to the street below them. Thousands of civilians were crowded into the square to await the arrival of their new leader, and with good reason. During his campaign, the man they elected had promised to rid the government of corruption and to arrest anyone who had accepted bribes. More important, he had promised to drive out the drug dealers, who had sold their poison to both the locals and the Americans who came to vacation in the island republic. The people were expecting great things from this man.

BOLAN HAD TRIED to convince the president-elect's advisers to insist the newly elected head of the state use an armored limousine the American government was willing to fly in for the parade.

"It would disappoint the people who threw the criminals out of power and elected our new president," Colonel Amirez explained, rejecting the recommendation.

The new president, Felipe Mayaguez, had run against the old regime that had been backed by South American cocaine interests. Despite many attempts on his life during the bitter campaign, the former Beruba Supreme Court judge had stood fast on his promise to throw the drug dealers out of the small Caribbean nation.

There was a long list of reforms the new president had pledged to institute, starting with universal education and government-backed treatment for those already addicted to drugs.

Watching as the presidential convertible turned into Avenida Libertad, the main street in front of the presidential palace, Bolan kept studying the crowds through his binoculars.

The police had stopped all traffic leading into the square and were scanning the crowds, searching for troublemakers.

Except for the new Mercedes-Benz stopped in the middle of the street north of the square, nothing seemed out of place.

The handsomely uniformed guards, the plumes on their helmets fluttering in the soft breeze, acted as a human shield.

Bolan studied the faces of the guards. Something bothered him, but he couldn't put his finger on what had aroused his suspicion.

"There," he snapped to the military man at his side. "That guard." He pointed to the uniformed man closest to the president-elect.

"I see nothing," Amirez replied, staring at the guardsmen.

The uniformed guard standing next to the presidential car had moved one of his hands under his uniform jacket. As the Executioner watched through the telescopic sight, a small bulge appeared in the otherwise perfect-looking uniform.

Without a word, Bolan leaned his eye against the scope and moved his finger to the SR-25's trigger. As the guardsman's hand came out from under his jacket, the big American could see the butt of a 9 mm Heckler & Koch P-9 S.

Bolan squeezed the trigger.

To the horror of the crowd, the guard dropped the pistol and grabbed his suddenly chinless face before falling to the ground.

MARGARITTA SCHINDLER looked stunned. Sitting next to the former Stasi assassin in the back of the Mercedes-Benz, she pointed to where the new president's touring car had stopped.

"Your man has been taken out," she stated, "before he could get even one shot off. What happened?"

"It doesn't matter," said the hard-faced man holding the M-14 carbine. A powerful scope was mounted where the open sights had been, and an M-203 grenade launcher was slung beneath the barrel.

"All that matters is that we complete the contract," he murmured as he opened the window and poked out the weapon.

The woman looked bewildered. In her years of killing, she had never assassinated a victim without having an escape route available.

"Are you crazy? The streets are filled with people and cars. Where will we go afterward?"

The gunman turned to the driver. "You heard the lady, Ricki. How do we get away?"

The ferret-faced man behind the wheel smiled icily. "The car will act as a battering ram. Anyone in our way will die."

THROUGH HIS BINOCULARS, Amirez stared at the dead guardsman, then turned to the big American.

"How did you know, Señor Belasko?"

Before he could reply, Bolan saw the muzzle of a carbine poke out of a side window of a Mercedes-Benz 500 stopped by the traffic police at the intersection.

He swung the SR-25 at the German-built car, but before he could get the vehicle in focus, he heard the whine of a fragmentation grenade and the violent explosion as it landed in the rear of the president's touring car, blowing up the president, his wife and a dozen guardsmen near the official vehicle.

The carbine poured a steady stream of 7.62 mm lead into the bodies of traffic police and pedestrians as the driver of the car tried to escape.

Bolan could see the face of the gunman through his sight, a hard-faced, balding man with the deadened expression of a professional.

There was a woman in the seat next to him, a platinum blonde with an equally expressionless face. He could see her staring at him, or, at least, at the rooftop from which he had killed the disguised assassin.

Behind the steering wheel was a swarthy, grinning jackal.

Bolan knew the Mercedes was more than a thousand feet away from the rooftop. But quickly swinging the sniper's rifle ahead of the assassin's getaway car, the soldier rapid-fired through the clip. Two rounds tore through the window and shattered the face of the gunman.

The car door opened and the blond woman shoved the corpse onto the roadway, then slammed the door and yelled something to the driver.

As the Mercedes-Benz vanished from his scope sight, Bolan heard a soft noise behind him, which he recognized immediately—the releasing of a pistol safety.

Calmly he pulled his finger from the SR-25's trigger and let it slip under the open zipper jacket he wore. As he turned, he saw the .45ACP Colt Government Model pistol in the colonel's hand and the angry expression on the man's face.

"You were in on the assassination all the time," Bolan stated.

"A half-million dollars is hard to refuse," the colonel replied, then added, "You are a very resourceful man, Señor Belasko. You would have found out about me in time.

Better for everyone if you were found dead. Somehow a third assassin gained access to the roof and killed you.''

"And you?''

"A slight bullet wound through the fleshy part of my hand will show how brave I was trying to fight back.''

"Wrong,'' the soldier replied, freeing the silenced 9 mm Beretta 93-R.

He stroked the trigger twice.

The first slug tore through the shocked colonel's open mouth. The second bore into his chest and chiseled its way to his heart muscle.

Amirez tried to speak but collapsed to the rooftop without uttering a word.

SCHINDLER WAS ANGRY at herself as she boarded the private jet to fly to New York. Her schedule would take her back to Corsica, where she could report to Marius on what she'd learned.

The wounds she had suffered were superficial. She had been wounded more severely on raids with the Baader-Meinhof Gang while in her youth.

The former Stasi assassin she had sat next to had taken all the slugs fired at the vehicle.

She had brought painkillers with her to deaden the boredom she thought she would suffer being merely an observer rather than a participant in the killings. Now she took the pills to relieve the temporary discomfort she felt.

The sniper who had killed the two assassins was a professional. She hadn't met many people who could have killed a man at that distance. She wished she could have seen him and studied the expression on his face.

She would have to use her contacts to find out who the mercenary was. The only thing she knew for certain was that he didn't work for the assassination contractor.

Not that she would put killing their own men past Lushenska and Hawthorne. She had known about their reputations when they were still with their governments' intelligence agencies—cold-blooded assassins, killing for a fee.

She understood such men, although she had always fought for a cause. But only because it made her feel righteous about murder.

The old juices Schindler hadn't felt in years began to flow through her body. She missed fighting for a cause. Any cause. She had fought alongside members of the Italian Red Brigades, the French Action Directe, the Palestinian Abu Nidal Faction and Baader-Meinhof.

Most of the groups had disbanded. The few that were left were being run by businessmen who were seeking to make a profit on the actions of their followers.

Schindler felt as if she had moved into a time warp, living in a period in history where there were no causes, no purpose to life.

Her raison d'être these days was to make sure that the killings Marius had ordered were carried out.

She could have conceived a much better assassination plot.

Her mind returned to the argument she had had with Marius the night before she left Corsica. They had made love—he passionately, she passively.

To her it was just part of the job. The only romance in her life was with death, especially those she caused.

Why should Marius spend a huge sum hiring an outside contractor when she was available?

She would have to discuss it with him again.

2

Thomas Fallon, the Central Intelligence Agency's chief of station at the American Embassy in Porto Santos, had been ordered by Washington to clear out a private office for Mike Belasko's use. Staring at the big man who stood before him, carrying a canvas carryall, the government representative wondered who Belasko really was.

He was impressively tall, more than six foot two, and looked like he weighed around two hundred pounds. But even with clothes on, Fallon could sense the man was all hardened muscle.

Belasko's expressionless eyes caught his attention. There was no anger, no curiosity, nothing, yet the graveyard stare missed nothing.

Fallon decided that his visitor was a member of some supersecret agency, and it made the CIA field official angry to have a government hit man on the premises of his embassy.

He had heard reports that Belasko had been responsible for the deaths of the two assassins. Now the press would hound him for information, while the ambassador, a political appointee, found some excuse to return to the United States until the press found something else to write about. The irritated intelligence official led the man into the large room, then slammed the door behind him as he left.

BOLAN SET DOWN the canvas carryall that contained his traveling arsenal and dialed the number that would route him to Hal Brognola's private phone after going through a series of cutouts.

When he had the big Fed on the line, Bolan reviewed the events of the past two hours.

"We've got a line on the dead assassin," Brognola stated.

"Already?"

"He was in the CIA computer files so it was easy to get a facial match on him."

"Who was he?"

"Kurt Weigrad. He was a top-level hit man with the East German Stasi until that group was disbanded."

"So he was freelancing."

"It would seem so," the head of Stony Man Farm replied. "Funny thing is the last information we had on Weigrad was that he was either dead or dying of cancer. I suppose he wanted to go out in a blaze of glory. There was no way he could have escaped."

"How about the man and woman in the car?"

"No hard match on the man. You didn't leave enough of his face to put together a composite. The CIA's taking his fingerprints. Maybe we'll get lucky."

"And the woman?"

"Nothing specific. Just some speculation on her."

"What kind of speculation?"

"One of the old-timers at the CIA used to be stationed in Berlin. At the time he was there, there was a blonde who had the same general appearance as the woman you saw. She was a high-level hit woman with the Baader-Meinhof Gang until it became the Red Army Faction and she disappeared."

"Does she have a name?"

"Margaritta Schindler. But my guess is that she's probably using an assumed name.

"If it is Schindler, she's a psychopath. Her father headed up one of the large German banks until she led a band of assassins to kill him, her mother and two sisters."

"Any lead on what she's been up to lately?" Bolan inquired.

"She moved from terrorist group to terrorist group for a number of years, then she vanished. A French Intelligence officer saw someone who looked like her at the film festival in Cannes a few years ago in the company of a man named Alexander Marius."

"Should I know his name?" Bolan asked.

"You might want to remember it. Marius is the head of the Union Corse."

"The Corsican Mafia?" Bolan whistled. "That's a switch for the Schindler woman. From terrorist to thug."

"There's no hard proof that the two of them hadn't just met in Cannes, or that she was trying to worm her way into the Corsican's organization." The head of Stony Man Farm remembered something. "This Marius is supposed to be trying to organize an international crime cartel with some of the biggest organized hoods in the world. The Yakuza in Japan, one of the big-league Triads in Hong Kong, the American Mafia, the investment adviser to a bunch of the Iranian-backed terrorist groups operating out of Lebanon and so on."

"Right now I'm more interested in finding out who hired the assassins to kill Mayaguez and his wife," Bolan stated.

"Don't make light of Marius. He and his group may have some involvement in those murders, although there's no hard evidence." Brognola paused. "But in answer to your question, someone who looked like Weigrad was in Bolivia last week, renting a car and asking directions to the Beni Lowlands."

"Isn't that a stronghold of the Bolivian cocaine cartel?"

"Exactly. They had a lot at stake. Mayaguez had promised to drive out the drug dealers if he was elected, and what's a few million bucks paid to pro killers when you've got a market that's worth fifty million a year?''

The Executioner thought about Amirez's comment that he'd been paid a half-million dollars for his part in the plot.

''They've made their last political donation,'' Bolan replied grimly.

Now it was time for them to meet their fate.

And if the platinum blond woman was actively involved, she would, too.

3

Corsica

Alexander Marius was concerned with the decline in profits, but he was careful not to let that concern show on his face.

Inviting some of the major worldwide criminal organizations to join him in taking control of a large number of arms-and-weapons-manufacturing companies had sounded like a rare opportunity to reap huge profits when the private company had been formed. But now, with the Cold War only a memory and warfare limited to a few places in the world, the organization was faced with a continuing loss of invested capital.

Marius was accountable only to the other organizations. Although he didn't run a democratic cartel, he did have powerful men who expected to earn a handsome profit from their various criminal ventures.

As head of the notorious Union Corse—the Corsican-based crime syndicate that controlled criminal activities in France and many of its neighboring countries—Marius was accustomed to negotiating with other criminal elements for joint ventures. But as he looked at the seven men seated at the long antique conference table, it was obvious that they wanted a full explanation of why the arms syndicate in which the criminal groups they represented had invested so much capital was losing money.

And what Marius planned to do about it.

The Japanese man to his right, Tojo Fujimoto, had been sent to the arms syndicate by two of the major Yakuza organizations.

Next to him, the elegantly dressed Chinese man, Wu Shu-Shei, was there to protect the investment made by the Chiu Chao Triad, one of the largest distributors of heroin from the Golden Triangle area of Southeast Asia.

Across from the Orientals sat a bulky, swarthy man, Razid Mansour, who kept an eye on the Turkish opium cartel's nonnarcotic investments.

The bearded Lebanese, Saloman Moussad, was the delegate of a number of Middle Eastern terrorist groups who used their profits from the arms syndicate to finance their war against Israel and the United States.

The thick-featured man sitting next to Moussad looked more Italian than American, but as Marius knew, Salvatore Gamboni was a key leader in the American Mob.

The thin-lipped man who had moved his chair away from Gamboni's was Hans Zelnick, the delegate of Latin American drug cartels, who kept their money in the Geneva bank he headed. They expected him to invest their money, to launder the primarily American hundred-dollar bills and to substantially increase the value of their bank accounts. For this the gray-haired banker got two percent of the profit he earned his clients.

It was a huge sum of money, which he cleverly concealed from the eyes of overmoralistic banking officials.

Next to Marius sat Philip Cambridge, who was representing a South African diamond-and-gold-mining syndicate.

He could sense their discomfort sitting in the library-turned-conference-room. It looked like the inside of an ancient cathedral into which somebody had placed a long oak table and chairs. There was something almost holy—too holy for the business they were discussing—about the room. Perhaps it was the concave ceiling, set two stories above and covered with frescos of Greek and Roman gods, or the long stained-glass windows set into the thick stone outer walls. Their discomfort gave Marius the slight edge he needed to maintain control.

But now he needed more than a religious setting to dominate the syndicate. He had called in a scapegoat who would at least momentarily satisfy their frustrations—the sales director of the arms-and-weapons combine, Phillipe Bouvier.

Looking at the nervous Belgian seated a few feet away from the table, Razid Moussad asked, "How much are sales off?"

"Fifty percent on weapons and munitions. Seventy-five percent on tanks and aircraft," Bouvier replied nervously, rechecking the columns of numbers printed on the sheets he held in his shaking hands.

Now came the crucial question.

"You have spent most of your life selling weapons and munitions to governments and private organizations. Why can't you sell the things our factories manufacture?"

"The times are different. There is no longer a Cold War. The American government has convinced many nations to rely on peaceful methods to resolve their differences," the sales director answered, sounding apologetic.

Marius looked at the expressions on the faces of the men around the table. They ranged from disgust to anger.

"What about the rebel forces? Certainly they are still purchasing arms," Moussad commented.

"The President of the United States has sent envoys to discuss compromise and has indicated his government is willing to help them obtain some of their demands if they will refrain from warfare."

The Middle Easterner looked skeptical. "Even the Iranians?"

"They are able to purchase whatever they need at bargain prices from the Russian military, who steals them from government warehouses," Bouvier replied, trying to hide his obvious fear.

Marius pulled at his earlobes as he listened. He was sure that Bouvier had done the best he could, but failure had to be punished.

He turned to the attractive, icy-featured platinum blond woman who sat behind him and nodded.

She nodded back, then stood and straightened her Parisian skirt. Picking up her long-strapped leather handbag, she slung it across a shoulder.

"Thank you, Mr. Bouvier. Miss Shimmel will see you out," the Union Corse leader said in French.

The stocky man gathered his papers and rose, his hands quivering.

No one said anything until Bouvier had left the conference room, led out by the blonde.

"Obviously an incompetent," the Swiss banker commented.

Marius didn't reply. Margaritta Schindler was a skilled bed companion, but she was even better at what he had hired her to do.

A pair of soft, muffled noises sounded from the hallway.

"Not any longer," he said with a half smile.

The blonde returned and took her seat again.

Marius rang a soft bell, which summoned one of his housemen. The Corsican smiled at him.

"It's too lovely a day to have the windows closed, Germain. Let's open them."

Without a word, Germain found a long wooden pole and pushed open the upper panels. The sounds and smells of late spring poured into the conference room.

Outside, the countryside was flourishing with new growth. The entire island looked like a florist's heaven.

Thousands of acres of maquis, the aromatic wild under-brush, smothered the pastures. Through the opened windows, the men could see the small coves far below the castle and in them the yachts of the wealthy who had made Corsica a second home.

The representatives of the various crime syndicates had seen the wild beauty of the large island on previous visits. The arms syndicate had been operating for the past five years, and most major meetings were convened there.

The rock castle that sat near on the slopes of Mount Cinto, the highest peak on the island, had been the ancestral home of the Marius family for five hundred years. From its stone rooms orders flowed for weapons and munitions to the more than a dozen factories the syndicate controlled. And the income generated was directed to offshore banks that were willing to launder the funds.

"An unusually beautiful day," Marius commented.

Then he addressed the large Corsican who had stood beside him throughout the early part of the meeting. "Jacques, get some men to help you get rid of the body in the hallway."

The servant nodded, then waited for more-specific instructions.

"The sharks looked particularly hungry when I was sailing yesterday."

The servant nodded again. He knew what he was supposed to do. He had done the same thing often in the past with rebellious members of the syndicate, or those who had made the mistake of trying to stand up to the Union Corse.

The Turk waited for the man to leave the room, then leaned forward in his chair and glared at the chairman. "What are we going to do about this situation? My people have much money invested in this business."

"A drop in the bucket, Mr. Mansour, compared to what

you and your people earn from the sale of refined opium each year," Marius replied calmly.

"We do not like losing money on any investment," the Turk warned in a threatening tone.

"Then we'll have to find a solution," Marius said.

He leaned forward and stared in turn at the seven men seated around the table.

"Has anybody got a suggestion?"

The Lebanese stared back at the chairman. "It is obvious that the Americans are behind the demise of our venture. Some of my backers think they should be taught a lesson."

Marius stared back at him. "You mean the American President?"

"Yes."

"And what do you propose we do about it?"

"It is my suggestion that if he was dead, we would arouse old enmities among other countries."

Marius nodded. "You are suggesting we have him killed."

"According to the newspapers, he will soon be coming to Brussels to address a NATO conference. When would there be a better opportunity?"

The elderly Yakuza representative at the table rose to his feet. "Such a suggestion is outrageous. Killing the American President could start a trade war. My people control many large international companies in my country. We cannot afford such a conflict at the present time."

"It may even lead to the resumption of the Cold War," the Swiss banker added with a half smile.

"Exactly," Marius replied. "Can you think of anything that would be better for our business than that?"

The Japanese representative stayed on his feet. "My group would never agree," he shouted.

Marius studied the diminutive figure. "If you want out,

just say so. I'm sure we can arrange for your group to withdraw from the syndicate, Mr. Fujimoto.''

"I can assure you they do."

"Perhaps you should leave before we continue our discussions." Marius turned to the platinum blonde. "Make arrangements for someone to drive Mr. Fujimoto to the airport.''

She smiled coldly as she stood and walked out of the conference room.

The Middle Easterner started to speak.

"One moment, Mr. Moussad," Marius said.

SCHINDLER SMILED at the distinguished-looking Japanese man.

"I am sorry you decided to withdraw from the syndicate," she said quietly.

"Perhaps it is better for everyone that I have. My people joined the group to make money, not to kill people. Especially someone as powerful as the American President.''

"Well, have a pleasant trip," she replied, and reached into her purse.

"Thank you. I am certain I will." Fujimoto turned to the front door of the castle.

"Oh, Mr. Fujimoto," the woman called.

The Japanese turned and saw the 9 mm Walther P-88 pistol, fitted with a silencer, that Schindler held in her hand.

He looked at her and started to ask a question, but the two slugs she unleashed tore into his skull before the words could come from his mouth. Then she turned to the two Japanese bodyguards who had been protecting him and emptied her pistol into them.

"I am sure the three of you will have a good trip. Wherever you are going," she said softly to the corpses sprawled on the floor.

Schindler turned to the husky thug standing guard in the foyer.

"The Mediterranean," she told him. "Make it look like his limousine ran off a narrow road along the edge of the island."

She started to turn away, then remembered something. "And send a message of condolence to his Yakuza partners in Japan."

MARIUS WAITED until he heard a pair of dull thuds echoing from the hallway.

"Now, is there anyone else who wishes to withdraw?"

The members of the syndicate's board of directors looked at one another with discomfort, but remained silent.

As Schindler reentered the conference room, the Union Corse chieftain studied the face of each of the men seated at the conference table.

"Given our new action plan, I suggest we order our managers to meet with us and instruct them to bring production up to their full capacity." He thought about it. "Given that it is spring, I know the hotel my group owns in the Alps is empty." He thought for a moment, then announced his decision. "We'll bring them to the hotel."

The Chinese Triad representative voiced his concern. "Is that wise—asking them to start increasing production?"

"It will take time to rebuild inventories," Marius replied.

"But what if they ask why the board is suddenly feeling so confident about the future?"

The Corsican smiled coldly. "I believe the men I have sent to protect our investments in each of the companies will make sure no such questions are asked."

Smiles replaced the nervous expressions on the faces of the other board members. They knew from previous reports what kind of men the Union Corse leader had sent to oversee the manufacturing plants—tough, cold-blooded professionals who settled disagreements with whatever gun they were carrying.

"One last piece of business before we adjourn. The American President's death. It cannot look like he died of natural causes. It must be obvious that somebody had arranged for his assassination, preferably a foreign government."

He looked at the Lebanese.

"Are you suggesting the blame be placed on Tehran?" The Middle Easterner shook his head. "Naturally they would like an enemy of God killed...."

The Corsican turned away from Moussad before he could complete his thought, and looked at each board member. Each had a blank expression on his face. Sighing, Marius turned to Schindler.

"Did you check out the Swiss group, Margaritta?"

The blonde looked annoyed as she leaned over and whispered in the Union Corse leader's ear. "I've asked you not to call me that in front of others," she reminded him in a suddenly hard voice. "Do you remember the name I am currently using?"

Marius whispered back. "Of course. Mathilde Shimmel."

The woman relaxed. "Please use it," she said as she gave his question thought.

"Perhaps this should be kept within this group. I believe we can handle it ourselves," she continued, then waited for Marius's reaction.

He weighed her suggestion, then shook his head. "No. We cannot afford to have such an act traced back to us."

The woman looked disappointed.

Marius turned to the banker. "I believe you have a report to present, Herr Zelnick."

The man nodded. "As you requested, Miss Shimmel and I met with a group of former intelligence officers in Switzerland. They employ only trained professionals in carrying out their assignments.''

"How good are they, and how discreet? Again we can't afford to have our name brought into this," Marius insisted.

"As Miss Shimmel knows, one of my clients recently hired them. She accompanied field agents of the group on that assignment," Zelnick replied.

"As you suggested," Schindler commented, giving her attention to the Corsican, "I went along on the mission Herr Zelnick just mentioned. They did complete their contract. Of course, they lost the two men they had sent to do the work."

"But the person they were hired to kill is dead," the Swiss banker reminded her.

The platinum blonde nodded. "The president of Beruba is dead," she admitted.

Marius stared into space, then turned to the banker. "Since you introduced this group as a possible resource for getting rid of competition, or potential enemies, tell us about them."

"There are two partners. One is a former Russian Intelligence director. The other is an American. I believe he held a senior position with the Central Intelligence Agency before he was retired."

The Union Corse chieftain weighed the information. "Since the group still doesn't know who we are, I would like it kept that way. Miss Shimmel and you should get to know them a little better before we hire them to undertake this assignment."

The banker nodded.

The American Mafia representative snapped an angry question. "How expensive are these people?"

"For an assignment like this, I would guess they would charge four or five million dollars, U.S.," Zelnick answered.

Gamboni sputtered his reply. "That's outrageous! We've never paid half that much to have somebody bumped off."

Marius glared at Gamboni, then turned back to the Swiss banker. "How much was this group paid to kill the Caribbean President?"

"The fee ran in excess of two million dollars," Zelnick replied.

"It's not really outrageous when you measure the profits we will gain if a war starts," Marius said to the American capo.

Then he turned to Schindler. "You and Herr Zelnick fly to Geneva and meet with the heads of the group. If we decide to engage them, I would like you to be their contact."

Schindler smiled. As a former member of the Baader-Meinhof terrorist group, she had missed the excitement of being involved in a political killing.

Especially a target as powerful as the President of the United States.

4

San Borja, Bolivia

Bolan jerked the steering wheel of the jeep sharply to the right. On the roof of the nearest building a swarthy man dressed in army-style fatigues aimed a Russian-made RPG-16 portable rocket launcher at the surplus military vehicle.

The rooftop assailant had a PG-7M HEAT rocket loaded in the launcher pressed against his shoulder. With a muzzle velocity of 120 meters per second, the 2.25-kilogram missile was capable of penetrating 3307 millimeters of armor, which was many times thicker than the bodywork of the jeep Bolan was driving.

The soldier stepped hard on the brake, then jumped from the vehicle, gripping an M-16 A-2 assault rifle in his hands. He rolled across the steep driveway that led to the mountaintop complex, then twisted to face the startled hardman above him and released a trio of 5.56 mm hollowpoints.

He knew that the M-16 A-2 was capable of pouring 800 rounds per minute at a muzzle velocity of 1000 feet per second with virtually no jamming, but the M-203 grenade launcher made it possible to hurtle a 40 mm grenade accurately as far as 400 meters.

The trigger finger of the rooftop guard pulled back as he dropped the weapon and grabbed for his shredded neck, trying to stop the blood gushing from his carotid artery, then fell over the edge of the roof and crashed on the concrete walkway below his post.

The launched HEAT missile climbed skyward at a slight angle, then turned and penetrated a thick stand of trees. Screams from the mangled bodies of hidden gunmen filled the still air for a few minutes.

Then came silence, as life rushed from them.

BOLAN HAD SLIPPED into Bolivia, then stole one of the surplus American jeeps from police headquarters in the administrative capital of La Paz.

He knew he would have to handle the assault alone. Calling on the federal police or military for assistance would be the same as calling the cocaine cartel and announcing his arrival. Many police and military officials were on the cartel's payroll. Not that every one of them had actively sought bribes. For every one who did, there were four who were forced to take them.

It was a matter of *plata o plomo,* "silver or lead." A man took the bribe and sold his soul, or took a bullet and died.

The graveyards were filled with those who didn't accept the bribe. The bars were crowded with those who did, trying to drink away their self-hate at succumbing to cowardice.

It had taken the Executioner almost a full day to make his way through Peru and then into Bolivia, traveling around Lake Titicaca to the city of Caranavi, and then to the Beni Lowlands. The most powerful of the Bolivian drug lords made his headquarters in an old mansion, surrounded by a number of smaller buildings, on the outskirts of San Borja, a small, dusty city that was once the center of cattle raising in Bolivia.

A call to Hal Brognola had gotten Mack Bolan the directions he needed to find the mansion of Carlos de Sonata, the major Bolivian cocaine grower.

And the man who had hired the assassins to kill President Mayaguez and his wife.

As he drove through San Borja, Bolan studied the faces of the men and women he passed on the streets. It was hard to believe that the humbled people who averted their eyes from him were the once-proud Aymara Indians who had been part of the Inca empire long before Pizarro and his Spanish soldiers turned them into slaves, forcing them to work the mines and great estates of the conquerors.

Even the few policemen he saw looked sheepish.

Starvation and subsistence farming had forced the populace into slavery again, working for starvation wages for the cocaine barons as farmhands and guards.

THE MANSION'S OPULENT living room was filled with antiques, relics of Carlos de Sonata's ancestors. As he sat facing the neatly dressed Russian, the Bolivian businessman asked a question.

"Why should I pay your organization when your men botched the assassination, Señor Krushenkov?"

"Mr. Sonata..." the Russian started to reply.

"*De* Sonata," the Bolivian snapped.

"Mr. de Sonata," the former KGB officer continued, "you hired us to kill the new president of Beruba. Mayaguez is dead. The contract has been fulfilled."

"But in such a way as to possibly attract attention to my people."

"What the police found were two professional gunmen, one from Romania, the other from Italy. There is nothing to connect them to you."

The Bolivian looked puzzled. "Who could have found out about your men? And about Colonel Amirez? We had many government officials receiving financial gifts from our people.''

Krushenkov wanted to collect the balance of the fee and leave. It was a long drive to the airport, and the worst part of his current occupation was having to indulge in idle chit-chat with clients.

As a senior member of the KGB until the fall of the Russian empire, Krushenkov had relied on his 9 mm Makarov PM pistol to deal with those who opposed him. But the position he held with the organization demanded that he use diplomacy first when he came to collect their fee. Violence was always the last resort.

''And what about your men? You don't seem the least bit concerned that they are dead,'' the Bolivian commented.

''They understood the risks when they accepted the assignment.''

''And this man who killed them? What about him?''

''He will be found and executed. But that is our business, not yours.''

''Are you sure? From what I've read, he was sent by the Americans to protect the president-elect.''

''He wasn't successful, was he?''

''Who was he?''

''He calls himself Mike Belasko,'' Krushenkov replied impatiently. ''That probably isn't his real name, but it is only a matter of time before we find him. His name won't matter then.''

The Russian checked his wristwatch. ''I have a plane to catch in two hours. So if there is nothing else, I will take our fee and leave.''

De Sonata started to offer a lesser sum, then examined the face of the Russian and changed his mind. He reached down and picked up a large leather case.

''Let me help you with that,'' the Russian offered, reaching for the heavy satchel. As he picked it up, the two men heard gunfire from outside.

The Russian looked startled. "What was that?"

"Intruders. Perhaps some foolhardy members of the police or military who refused my gifts and have chosen to die as heroes instead." The Bolivian smiled. "Perhaps mercenaries sent by our competitors in Colombia." He shrugged. "It doesn't matter. I have more than a dozen armed professionals watching this house."

He stood.

"Come outside," he told his visitor, "and watch how we handle unwanted guests."

A QUARTET of hard-faced men appeared from behind the mansion.

Bolan had shouldered the M-16 and replaced it with an Uzi submachine gun. The Israeli-made weapon was better for the close-in combat the Executioner knew was ahead of him.

He slipped behind a stone building housing the cars and trucks used by the cocaine dealer and his men, studying the faces of the gunmen. These weren't local Indians pressed into service. These were professionals, hired guns recruited from the streets of Colombia, Mexico and the United States.

Each carried a 7.62 mm AK-47 carbine. As Bolan knew from prior missions, the Russian-made Kalashnikovs were excellent weapons. Fitted with 30-round magazines, the assault rifles could unleash 800 rounds per minute.

The soldier stepped into the open and, as the startled gunners brought up their weapons, he hosed them with a sustained burst of 9 mm parabellum rounds.

The four men collapsed to the ground in a tangled heap without getting off a shot.

A fatigue-clad gunman popped up from behind one of

the trucks, a 5.45 mm RPK-74 light machine gun clenched in his hands. The man looked German rather than Latin.

Another mercenary, Bolan decided as the hardman lifted the machine gun and pointed it at the warrior.

Waiting until the mercenary's finger moved toward the trigger, Bolan executed a rapid twist toward the gunman, rather than away from him. Startled by the unexpected move, the German assailant tried to adjust his aim.

But Bolan cut loose with the Uzi, stitching a figure eight from left to right across the gunner's midsection.

The mercenary dropped his weapon and tried to hold his stomach shut, but his oozing intestines pushed their way over and under his quivering hands. Dying, he fell forward onto his face on the hard-packed dirt.

Quickly Bolan dropped the empty magazine from the well and rammed home a full one, setting the fire selector switch to the 3-round-burst mode.

The Israeli subgun was a solid fighting tool. The Uzi weighed less than seven and a half pounds and was only seventeen inches long, from the tip of its short snub barrel to the end of its folded metal stock. Each magazine held twenty-five rounds of high-velocity ammo, and the weapon could be fired one handed when necessary.

Nine millimeter parabellum rounds hurtled out of the barrel at the rate of 600 rounds per minute, with a velocity of 1,250 feet per second. Changing magazines took split seconds.

Four more men armed with AK-47s poured out of the barn and, goaded by a fifth man behind them, rushed the Executioner.

There was no time to take aim. He sectored off each attacker and pumped lead until all five were dead or dying.

Another group of men started to run toward him, then stared in horror at the bodies strewed around the grounds. Turning, they raced toward the deep woods, flinging the

AK-47s to the ground to signal Bolan they weren't willing to fight him.

Now it was time to meet their employer.

Changing magazines again, Bolan moved up the front steps of the main house, alert to any sign of ambush.

The front door opened and two men started to come out, stopping abruptly when they spotted Bolan.

Krushenkov started to reach for the Makarov pistol in the belt holster under his jacket.

Bolan remembered the Russian from a previous assault on KGB headquarters in Moscow.

As he recalled, the man was expert with guns.

A gentle tug of his trigger finger sent three rounds flying toward the ex-KGB agent's throat. The first missed by a fraction of an inch. The other two severed arteries near the Russian's throat.

Krushenkov dropped his pistol and grabbed at his neck, refusing to fall down.

"You can't stop all of us," he gasped. "We are too many."

"Who are 'we'?"

The Russian grinned, and a mouthful of blood bubbled from between his lips. He slid to the ground, letting go of the large satchel he carried.

The latch opened, and neat stacks of American currency spilled out.

As de Sonata dived to one side and raised a .357 Smith & Wesson revolver, Bolan cut loose with the Uzi, catching the cocaine cartel leader high in the chest, pulverizing his heart.

The Executioner gathered up the satchel of money to add to his war chest, knowing it would come in handy in the next phase of his mission.

5

Geneva, Switzerland

Nate Hawthorne looked up from the stack of reports on his desk. The tweedy pipe smoker who'd just wandered into his office was his partner, Viktor Lushenska.

He was amused. The former Russian general looked more like a tall, lanky American college professor than the former head of the directorate that ran the KGB's teams of "wet workers"—the euphemism for assassins.

There was a sour expression on Lushenska's face.

"Anything wrong?"

"Everything. We've got to be more selective in whom we hire." He lit his pipe. "Those two clumsy oafs we sent to Beruba got themselves killed."

Hawthorne looked surprised. "So the new president is still alive."

"No, they got him before somebody shot them."

"Good. Then we still collect our fee. Why worry about them? There are still plenty of unemployed intelligence agents who would like to work for us."

"Alexander Marius, the head of the Union Corse, sent an observer, that blond woman, to check us out," Lushenska snapped. "We looked like a bunch of amateurs."

The former CIA Latin American chief of operations shook his head. "Not good. A good job there was essential to our landing a second well-paying hit."

The Russian nodded. "The American President."

Hawthorne looked puzzled. "Why would someone like Alexander Marius want to kill the President?"

"You should use your friends more, Nate," Lushenska said, a small smile turning up the corners of his lips. "The Corsican is heading up a syndicate of foreign crime cartels who have acquired a network of small-arms manufacturers around the world. The relative lack of wars—compared to the days when I was with the KGB—is hurting the group financially."

The American understood immediately. "Kill the President and lay the blame on some foreign government, or group, and the Cold War resumes. Good thinking on Marius's part." Hawthorne leaned back in his leather chair. "We still may get the assignment. Who else would undertake such an action?"

He then changed the subject. "Do we know who took out our men?"

"According to the last report from Krushenkov, it was an American named Michael Belasko. I expect you to have someone find him, Nate. He's most likely CIA."

There was something about the former KGB general that made the smartly dressed American uncomfortable. At first glance he seemed mild enough, and his voice sounded like that of an elderly professor past retirement, who liked to lecture his people.

But Lushenska's eyes were the giveaway. They were cold and expressionless, the eyes of a stone killer. And nobody could have survived the series of purges of the KGB without being hard and shrewd.

Right now the former CIA official was more concerned with their Latin American clients, not the sniper who had taken out their men.

Even when he was with the Company, Nate Hawthorne had maintained discreet contact with the heads of the various criminal cartels, preparing for when he would retire and conduct business with them.

Like the Bolivian cartel run by Carlos de Sonata. Hawthorne had made it possible for the Bolivians to bring their cocaine across the border and the borders of neighboring countries in exchange for help in some clandestine hit.

Sometimes a client recommended him to another client, such as Hans Zelnick, who handled money-laundering investments for the Bolivians.

Zelnick had arranged for Hawthorne and Lushenska to meet with the attractive blond woman who represented an arms syndicate.

The fee that Hawthorne had quoted for taking out the U.S. President was reasonable in his estimate—four million dollars. It wasn't an exorbitant sum when her superiors realized the difficulty of reaching the man they wanted killed.

He stopped thinking about the potential profits Lushenska and he could earn. Now he had to contact de Sonata and make sure he was satisfied with their services.

He turned to the Russian. "I'll find out everything I can about Belasko, Viktor," he promised.

The tweedy man seemed satisfied with the reply. "I know you will. I'd expect no less from the man I made my partner."

Before the retired CIA officer could reply, Lushenska turned and left.

As Hawthorne started to reach for the phone on his desk, it rang. He picked up the receiver.

It was Zelnick, and he sounded angry.

"We should talk right away," Zelnick said.

"I'll call you back."

Switching his scrambler, the CIA official dialed Zelnick's private number and waited for him to answer.

"Have you heard from de Sonata?" Zelnick demanded.

"No. I didn't expect to hear from him. I was going to call and make sure he was satisfied with our services."

"I have been trying him all day. Nobody answers his telephone."

There was a pause.

"De Sonata never leaves his estate. Something is wrong," the banker said, sounding worried.

"I'll be hearing from the man we sent to collect our fee. Perhaps the two of them drove to a nearby city to celebrate over a leisurely meal."

"I hope you are right," Zelnick snapped. "He invests a considerable sum of money through us."

"I'll call you when I reach de Sonata or hear from our man," Hawthorne promised.

As he replaced the receiver on the telephone base, the retired CIA executive began to think of the other contract agents he had on his string. He wondered if he should contact one of them and have him check out the situation.

THE BANKER HUNG UP the phone, then slammed his fist onto the highly polished desk in his antique-filled private office. The antique Rosenthal coffee cup jumped out of its saucer and crashed to the hardwood floor.

Zelnick stared down at the front page of the *New York Times*, which he had thrown onto the floor earlier. The major story was the killing of Mayaguez, and there wasn't a hint of any link to de Sonata.

He knew he had to keep trying to call de Sonata. After all, millions of dollars invested by the Bolivian were at stake.

De Sonata might not express any anger, but Zelnick knew it would be there, hidden behind a mask of understanding and sympathy. Just as he had sounded so understanding when the banker had called him to report that the arms syndicate had suffered additional financial losses.

Much of the money at risk belonged to de Sonata, who had backed Zelnick when he started his own international banking network ten years earlier.

For almost a decade since he had started his own banking system, Hans Zelnick had parlayed the illegal funds entrusted to him into huge fortunes. It was like second nature to him.

Zelnick's ancestors had been in banking for hundreds of years. Until his grandfather emigrated to Switzerland and changed his name, the banks they ran were located in tax havens throughout the world, in Eastern countries such as Bahrain, Yemen and Lebanon. Their customers were businessmen, sometimes involved in legal activities, at other times, not so legal.

Those who profited from drugs, gold smuggling, white slavery and money laundering were acceptable as depositors and borrowers to Zelnick's great-grandfather and the men who came before him. It was only in Switzerland, with its rigid banking laws, that such ventures were pilloried. He remembered being forced to resign from the major Geneva bank he'd been with for more than twenty-five years when they started suspecting him of laundering money for Carlos de Sonata and his competitors, the Medellín and Cali cartels.

Unofficially de Sonata functioned as a member of the board of the bank, with several of the other major investors. Naturally, with their public records, their names never appeared on any bank documents.

The bank had begun as a small laundering operation. But the profits his backers were earning from the sale of narcotics had begun to grow into the billions. They needed places to invest the money.

Zelnick remembered that first meeting in Baranquilla, Colombia, ten years earlier with de Sonata and the other investors.

"You can increase your incomes substantially—and legally—if the bank makes loans."

"To whom would you loan money?" Montoya, the representative of the Medellín group, had asked.

"Real-estate developers, manufacturers of chemicals and plastics, the larger defense contractors and gun manufacturers around the world. Companies like that," Zelnick answered.

"At what rate?" de Sonata, who represented the Bolivian cocaine growers, asked.

"As much as we can get. As an international bank, we aren't tied down by any one country's regulations," Zelnick replied.

"I think we should include revolutionaries who need money to finance their wars," the Bolivian suggested. "They're a good source of fighters if any of us ever need them."

"The good news is that I know of an international group of professionals who plan to organize an arms syndicate. They will buy up small, independent manufacturers and keep them busy with orders from the groups they represent," Zelnick added.

The plan had been approved unanimously, and de Sonata suggested that Zelnick protect the investments of his group by acting as a member of the board of directors of the new syndicate.

"It is only natural that a banker would be on the board of an international undertaking," de Sonata commented.

Zelnick started lending the laundered money. Ten million here, twenty million there, until he tapped into the international defense industry as their primary nonnarcotic source of profits.

By now more than one hundred million dollars had been invested in defense contractors around the world. As mutual

Jackal Hunt

distrust grew, so did their businesses. And Zelnick was right there, ready to lend them more money to expand.

Then, thanks to a weak-willed American President and a Russian president ready to sell his country's soul for peace, the investments were in danger of being lost. Knowing de Sonata, so was Zelnick's life.

The Swiss banker would have liked to spend his time reminiscing on the profits he had brought his clients rather than try the overseas call again.

He got up and looked out of the large window behind him. Eight stories below, the summer heat had raised tempers. Pedestrians were angrily scurrying up and down the avenues, while impatient drivers honked at one another on the crowded street.

He couldn't delay it anymore. He dialed the number in Bolivia.

There was still no answer.

Zelnick was tempted to call the Swiss ambassador in La Paz, but knew he couldn't. Word of his unusual interest would get back to Switzerland, and an investigation of his bank's operation could be conducted by the authorities.

The tall, impeccably dressed man was so tense, he wasn't aware that the delicate porcelain cup, which had been one of his mother's prized possessions, had broken into a hundred pieces on contact with the hard maple floor.

He glanced at the newspaper headline again. Beruba's President-Elect, Wife, Murdered.

The one thing he could feel good about was that the assassins had carried out their mission before they were killed, and that there was no mention of a possible connection to cocaine dealers.

As he waited for someone to answer de Sonata's private line, he could imagine the elegantly dressed, white-haired man who sat on the other end of the line calmly pondering if he was going to let Zelnick continue to sit on the board of the arms syndicate.

Or live.

Behind the benevolent exterior of the kindly grandfather, who took care of the residents of San Borja and the surrounding villages, was a powerful, unforgiving businessman. Zelnick had heard rumors of what happened to associates who betrayed him or, even worse, failed.

He was determined not to fall into either category.

The Swiss banker could sense that his banking empire was crumbling. All the years he had spent creating the image of a benevolent patriarch would be wasted if the bank failed. The donations he had made to the right causes, even the gifts he had donated to the government, without seeming to want anything in return—all were useless gestures now.

Zelnick placed the receiver on its cradle. He was so deep into his thoughts that he never heard the stout, middle-aged woman who was his secretary open the door to his office and walk in.

"Is everything all right, Herr Zelnick? I thought I heard a crash...." She stopped talking as she saw the bits and pieces of fine china on the floor. Quickly she knelt and began to push the pieces of the cup into a pile. She glanced up at the elegantly dressed man, who seemed so oblivious to the loss of a piece of rare porcelain.

"What happened, Herr Zelnick?"

He stared at her, surprised at her presence, then followed her eyes to the bits of china on the floor. "I don't know, Anna."

She stared helplessly at the cup. "The cup. It's...it's broken."

"Yes, it is." Some other time he would have been terribly upset. He liked touches that implied to visitors that he had come from an old, established family.

"Call some of the antique dealers," he suggested calmly. A broken cup—even one as rare as this—was a minor nuisance at the moment. "See if one of them can find a replacement."

She left the room to make the calls while the banker returned to the more important issue on his mind—making sure that his Bolivian client wasn't too upset at the turn of events in Beruba.

He remembered the vote by the arms board about the American President and the meeting with the woman from the organization.

Perhaps that would please de Sonata. He knew the Bolivian resented the problems the United States government had created for his couriers.

Zelnick decided to wait several hours before trying to call his client again.

6

Zelnick had tried to reach Hawthorne and Lushenska as soon as he heard the news.

Carlos de Sonata had been killed, along with a large number of his guards and a visiting Russian.

It was late and nobody answered the phones at their offices.

Finally he took a chance and called a contact at the government communications authority.

"It is urgent I reach either a Herr Viktor Lushenska or a Herr Nate Hawthorne. Both reside in the Geneva area."

"You bankers. Always working." The woman at the government offices laughed. "Did one of them pass a bad check?"

"No, no. Nothing like that, Miss Meissner. It has to do with their international business affairs."

That the woman understood, being Swiss. International business came first, before family and pleasure. It was the lifeblood of the country.

"There will be a handsome gift for you if you can help me."

Within ten minutes, the woman called Zelnick back on his private line and gave him both numbers.

"Of course, this never happened," she warned.

Suddenly he was more charming than he had been when he first contacted her. "But the gift will," he promised.

Then tried Hawthorne's number, with no success.

Zelnick would have preferred to pass the news along to the American, who seemed less ominous than his partner.

In desperation, he called the second number, and Lushenska answered.

Zelnick told him what he had just heard on the international news.

"Was there any mention of money being found?"

"Not a word. Should there have been?"

"No," the Russian hastened to assure the banker. "I was just curious."

Then he hung up the phone.

VIKTOR LUSHENSKA SAT in his den and weighed the information.

Krushenkov and the Bolivian were dead. The Russian courier had worked for him for many years, until the government had retired both of them.

Somebody had either accidentally found out that Krushenkov was meeting with the Bolivian to collect the large fee or they had been sent there.

Krushenkov had been an expert shot and a careful man. He would have been aware if he was being followed.

So it was reasonable to assume somebody had been waiting to ambush him.

But who?

The evidence pointed to the two men still alive—Hawthorne and himself. Since it wasn't he who had killed Krushenkov and the others, there was only one logical explanation.

Nate Hawthorne.

He knew that the American and his wife lived in a small village just outside the city, on a quiet lane along the Lac Léman, the famous lake of which the people of Geneva were justifiably proud.

It was time to dissolve the partnership.

For Krushenkov's sake, and his.

He lifted the telephone and dialed the private number of Kammil Agca, a man he used for personal assignments.

Agca had been one of field men in the KGB, and had been a high-ranking member of the Turkish terrorist gang before that.

The man was cold-blooded, but loyal.

THE DAWNING SUN STRUGGLED to climb into the eastern sky. It wasn't quite 5:00 a.m., and all the houses that rimmed Lac Léman were still dark.

The small panel van that moved slowly along the two-lane road paused occasionally while the uniformed driver studied the numbers on the houses they passed. The man sitting next to him also wore the uniform of a local messenger service.

The uniforms, like the van, were stolen. The men to whom the uniforms belonged were dead, killed the previous night as they were pulling into the messenger service garage. The impostors had dropped their weighted bodies into the lake on the way to Hawthorne's home.

The man next to the driver referred to a piece of paper in his left hand. "We're looking for number 239," he said for the third time since they'd turned onto the country road.

Anyone glancing at the vehicle would have assumed that one of their neighbors was receiving some important document that couldn't wait to be handled by their regular postman.

Had they been able to see inside the vehicle, they would have thought something different. The man seated next to the driver fondled a 9 mm Glock Model 18 selective-fire machine pistol, fitted with a sound suppressor. On the floor next to the driver was a silenced 9 mm Heckler & Koch MP-5 KA-5 submachine gun, loaded with hollowpoint cartridges.

Behind them a third uniformed man sat on a folding jump seat, cleaning an Ingram MAC-10 submachine gun, fitted with a long sound suppressor. He kept staring out of the side windows at the still lake as he pushed the cloth-tipped swab in and out of the stubby barrel. "It is too damned quiet around here," he complained.

"It will be noisy enough in a little while," the man next to the driver replied.

The driver turned the wheel slightly as the lane curved around the lake. There was a two-story wooden structure on the rim of the cul-de-sac ahead. The men in the van could see the black wrought-iron numbers nailed to the white wooden mailbox post. It was the address they wanted. The name painted on the old-fashioned mailbox was Hawthorne.

The killers had been told to eliminate everyone in the household.

"Keep the engine running," one passenger told the driver as he opened his door and got out, partially hiding the hand holding the Glock 18 submachine pistol under his opened jacket. He started to walk toward the front door when it opened. The third man slid the side door open and eased out, scanning the area as he gripped his weapon in his right hand.

The reddish blond man who stood in the doorway was still in his pajamas and robe. He signaled for the man to come closer. Lushenska had awakened him to ask if he had the bank resolutions for the partnership at home, and had told him to expect a courier to pick them up.

A woman's voice called out from inside the house. "Who's at the door, Nate?"

"Nobody, dear. Just a messenger from the office," he replied.

He turned, reached down and grabbed a slim leather briefcase.

"Tell Viktor I'll see him later in the office," he whispered, sounding annoyed, "and that I still don't understand why he needed these papers so damned early."

"Perhaps because you will no longer have any use for them," the uniformed man replied as he fired three rounds into Hawthorne's stomach.

Coils of intestines squirmed through the huge hole as Hawthorne fell forward.

The assassin reached down and started to pick up the attaché case when Hawthorne's wife came to the door, still tying her long, thin robe.

"Nate," she called out, "are you coming back to—?"

She saw the body on the ground, stared at the man holding the submachine pistol, then began to scream hysterically.

The thug leaning against the van swung his submachine gun toward her chest and fired off two rounds. The hollow-point bullets exploded into her lung, tearing away skin, tissues and blood vessels.

Unaware she was dying, the woman kept screaming until the blood from her ruptured vessels gagged her. She was still twitching as she fell to the ground.

The gunman stepped up to her fallen form and fired a third shot into her head, then watched until she stopped moving before he climbed back into the van.

As they raced back down the lane, the driver asked, "What time is it?"

The other man sitting up front checked his wristwatch. "Five-fifteen."

"Good. We're supposed to meet the client at the coffee shop on Rue des Alpes at five forty-five."

He checked in the rearview mirror. The road was empty. It had been a very simple assignment, compared to most Lushenska gave him, he thought as he slowed the van. No point getting a ticket now.

Two days later

THE FUNERAL for Nate Hawthorne and his wife, Molly, took place at eleven in the morning. Both caskets were closed.

Neither Hawthorne nor his wife had any immediate family except for his niece, Sally.

She sat at the edge of the graves, barely hearing the words of the visiting American minister. She was still in shock. Everything that happened after the police called her about their deaths was still a blur. She hadn't called anyone except her uncle's partner, Viktor Lushenska, to tell him about the murders.

Sounding shocked at the news, he promised to make all the funeral arrangements, then met her at the funeral home and promised to stay at her side as long as she needed him.

Now she sat near the coffins, dressed in a simple black dress, surrounded by members of Lushenska and her uncle's staff. Despite the constant outpouring of sympathy from the people in the firm, she heard very few of their words.

She knew what the firm's business was. She had worked for the CIA as a field agent in a number of American embassies. And when her uncle retired, she had accepted his offer to work as his personal assistant in the firm that he and his retired KGB associate had started.

That they dealt in death had never bothered her. By the time her uncle had retired, she had spent more than ten years participating in the deaths of America's enemies.

At thirty-four, she was already old. Until now the face of death had been merely part of the job, as it had been for her recently-dead uncle.

Tears wouldn't come. She had exhausted her supply when they closed the coffin lids of her uncle and aunt. All she could give the two who had raised her when her own parents had died in an automobile accident was the love and gratitude she had always had for them.

Lushenska, who was sitting next to her, kept looking around the cemetery. He suddenly stood and whispered he'd be right back. Sally turned her head and watched as he walked to an ancient-looking Mercedes-Benz 280 stopped in the cemetery drive. He leaned into the open rear car window and chatted with someone for a moment. Then he reached inside and took a slim leather portfolio from the person inside the vehicle.

As the Russian turned and walked back toward her, Sally recognized the leather case. It had belonged to her uncle. She could see dark stains on the leather, and they looked like dried blood.

The car began to move slowly toward the exit, and she caught a glimpse of the man driving. She recognized the brutish killer Lushenska had used for lower-level hits.

Kammil Agca.

Why was the Turk carrying her uncle's leather case, and how did he get it?

Lushenska looked like he had the answers to the questions suddenly flitting through her mind. She thought she knew the answers and became filled with a desire for revenge.

She decided to call Rudy Johnson. Her uncle had worked directly under the man for many years, and he had sent her a wire the minute he heard about the murders.

She had information she was positive he would want to know, and it concerned the planned assassination of the President of the United States.

7

Washington, D.C.

Most of the men seated in easy chairs in the Oval Office weren't familiar with the man the President had introduced as "Hal." Some of them had seen him at meetings with the President in the past, but usually only in times of extreme crisis. Only a few even knew his name was Harold Brognola.

Some of those present knew he used to be with the Federal Strike Force on Organized Crime, but none knew his current function.

Except for the President, no one else was aware that they were in the same room as the director of the Sensitive Operations Group, organized to counter the activities of international terrorists, dictators, organized-crime leaders and other threats to the United States of America.

Even fewer knew the identity of the man Brognola had brought to the meeting. The President hadn't thought it necessary to introduce him.

One of those who thought he knew who Brognola had brought to the meeting was Rudy Johnson, deputy director of operations for the Central Intelligence Agency. It was his job to find out the true identities of those he considered potential enemies of the United States, or of the CIA.

Brognola was high on the list, and so was a man named

Belasko, if he was, indeed, Belasko, the man who had taken out two assassins in Beruba.

This wasn't the time to bring up the subject. He had come at the request of the President, and waited for the Man to explain the reason for the urgent summons.

He didn't have to wait very long.

"As you know," the President said, "this administration has been successful in convincing many of our friends abroad that war wasn't the way to resolve differences they may have with other countries. We haven't always been successful—the conflict in what was once Yugoslavia, the international terrorism efforts backed by the Iranian government and so on. But for the most part, we have been successful enough that the sales volume of manufacturers of weapons and ammunition has fallen to an all-time low."

There was a polite smattering of applause at the announcement.

"I plan to continue the momentum we started in the direction of total disarmament around the world when I speak before the NATO council in Brussels. Unfortunately not everybody is thrilled with what I'm trying to accomplish."

He looked at the CIA representative, then continued.

"According to the CIA, there are rumors that there will be at least one organized attempt on my life while I'm in Europe. Let me emphasize that these are only rumors. The CIA hasn't been able to confirm them or identify any group that would make such an attempt."

Rudy Johnson had illusions of becoming the hero who saved the President, not forfeit that title to Brognola's mercenary.

He started to protest, but Brognola beat him with a question.

"How reliable are your sources?"

Johnson held back on identifying Sally Hawthorne. She was his source, not Brognola's.

"As I said, Mr. President, so far we only have rumors. But we believe that where there are rumors, there's a strong likelihood they're based on fact."

The President turned to Brognola.

"What do you think, Hal?"

"Fact or fiction, we ought to check it out, Mr. President."

The Man nodded. "I agree."

He turned to the others in the room. "I want any information on attempts to kill me given to me personally. I'll make sure Hal gets a copy immediately."

Johnson was suddenly livid. "The CIA is responsible for your safety abroad, Mr. President, as well as the White House detail of the Secret Service, of course," he reminded the President, trying to control the anger he felt.

In a calm voice, the man behind the large desk said, "Actually the Secret Service is, Rudy, but I'm sure that Hal will contact you whenever he needs your Agency's assistance."

"One more thing," a trim, gray-haired man said.

"What is it, Bob?"

"I would like to ship the armored limousine to Brussels. Just as a precaution."

Bob LaCross was head of the White House detail of the Secret Service. He and his team traveled everywhere with the President. As the Chief of State knew, they were sworn to sacrifice their lives to save his, and he knew that every man and woman in the detail would do so.

"I'll give you my answer in a few days, Bob," the President replied, then stood.

Following his lead, everyone in the Oval Office did so, too.

"The meeting is over, gentlemen." He then turned to Brognola.

"I'd like you and Mr. Belasko to stay."

"I'd like to speak with the deputy director for CIA operations," Bolan said.

The Chief Executive nodded.

The room emptied quickly. Finally the President, Brognola, Bolan and Johnson were alone.

"Who was the source you quoted in the meeting?" Bolan asked Johnson.

"Sorry, but that's classified."

"I'm asking the same question, Rudy," the President snapped.

Reluctantly the CIA official swallowed his pride. "One of them was a woman named Sally Hawthorne."

"Any relation to Nate Hawthorne?" Brognola queried.

Johnson nodded. "His niece. She left the Agency last year to take a job with her uncle. Nate Hawthorne had been a trusted member of the CIA for many years, until he retired several years ago and opened a consulting firm in Geneva."

"Didn't he get into trouble over the hiring of mercenary assassins?"

"A misunderstanding," Johnson replied blithely. "Everyone in the Agency has those who are jealous of our successes."

Bolan was about to reply, but Brognola stopped him with a touch on his shoulder.

"Didn't Hawthorne just get killed?" the big Fed asked.

Johnson nodded. "Hawthorne and his wife were murdered two days ago by a gang of thugs. Probably burglars who thought they were away and became frightened when they found them home."

Bolan picked up the questioning. "Why would Sally Hawthorne know anything about assassination attempts if she left the CIA?"

Johnson shook his head. "She was a trained agent. Perhaps she heard rumors in the field."

Bolan remembered the retired CIA official. One of his

functions had been to control the Latin American contract killers hired by the CIA. Then he thought of the Russian he had killed in Bolivia. The money he'd been carrying had been a large sum. A fee for killing the president-elect of Beruba?

"Or maybe that's what her uncle's firm does for a living—hires themselves out as assassins," Bolan suggested.

Johnson became incensed. "Hawthorne wouldn't be involved in contract killings. And I knew her uncle for many years. He abhorred killing, even when he was told it was necessary," he snapped.

Bolan held his skepticism in check. To call the CIA official a liar wouldn't solve anything.

The President turned to Johnson. "I don't think we need to keep you from your work any longer, Rudy. Thanks for coming on such short notice."

Johnson started to protest, then saw the hard expression on the Chief Executive's face. Without another word he stood and walked out of the Oval Office.

When they were alone, the President turned to Bolan. "Any thoughts, Striker?"

Bolan nodded. "I'll accept the mission, but I'll need your cooperation."

The President looked surprised. He had met Bolan on rare occasions in the past. This was the first time the man asked him to be involved.

"How?"

"For one thing, use the armored limousine. Another, let the Secret Service men and women form a shield around you."

The President smiled. "Sometimes that's difficult to do. I'm still a politician, and shaking hands is an important part of my job."

The soldier understood. "Do the best you can not to expose yourself to needless danger."

The Chief Executive nodded, and looked relieved. "Getting the assassins isn't enough," he warned.

"I agree," Brognola replied, then turned to Bolan. "We've got to stop whoever's behind the attempts."

"I've already figured that out," Bolan replied.

Then he remembered the platinum blond woman he had seen in the second assassin's car.

"I think I know one place to start my search."

The President looked puzzled.

"It's a long story," Bolan replied, "and I might be wrong."

But his gut told him that the head of the Union Corse was somehow involved. It was up to the Executioner to find out how.

8

Geneva

The ancient Mercedes exited an almost barren section of the ancient city and entered an unlit side road. There was no traffic on the narrow road at that hour, as Kammil Agca knew. He drove the vehicle into a shuttered gas station and stopped.

The Turk stared at his passenger, Sally Hawthorne. He had convinced her to get into his car as she was about to enter a small café, telling her he'd been sent by Lushenska, who knew why her uncle was killed and who was behind it.

When Hawthorne had dropped her guard and moved closer to Agca's car, the Turk had shoved a compact 9 mm Asp pistol into her chest.

Driving with one hand, the Turk kept his small pistol aimed at her until he had a chance to stop the car and handcuff Hawthorne's wrists behind her back. He also shoved a handkerchief into her mouth to prevent her from screaming.

He could see the mixture of terror and hate in her eyes. He was used to the blend of expressions. Most of the victims he had executed had the same look.

Agca was a heavyset man in his late thirties, with the dark features of his Turkish ancestors and a wide scar that cut across the left edge of his mouth, leaving him with a permanent smile. He had been an agent of the KGB before they laid off most of their field personnel.

He had worked for Lushenska's directorate as a field operative, and more than a hundred enemy agents and dissidents were buried in Turkish cemeteries because of him.

When Lushenska's department had moved him to Switzerland, the Turk thought he had been given the key to Paradise. Unlike Ankara, Geneva was a city filled with beauty and people who participated in keeping their community attractive.

The Paradise pass had been taken away when he was told by his control at the Russian embassy that, like many others in the intelligence service, he was now unemployed. When the retired Lushenska decided to base his private operation in Geneva, the former KGB general had contacted Agca and offered to give him freelance assignments. There weren't many, but each paid well.

Turning away from the American woman, the Turk thought of the money he would be paid for killing her. Feeling relaxed and satisfied, he reached into his pocket and treated himself to a rare pleasure, one of the Turkish cigarettes he had purchased at a local tobacconist.

As he inhaled the delicate perfume of the tobacco, he reached into a jacket pocket and took out a German-made cellular phone. Tucking the pistol inside his waistband, he checked his small telephone book and found the number he was seeking. He dialed it, punching the Send button at the end.

He waited, listening as the phone kept ringing. Then he heard the familiar voice on the other end.

"We're here, just outside the city," Agca said. "What do you want me to do?"

Lushenska had told him to call before he carried out the killing of Sally Hawthorne. The Russian wanted to find out who she had called in the United States and, if possible, what she had said.

The Russian's contact in the CIA confirmed she had called and asked for Rudy Johnson, deputy director of operations.

"I think she called to tell him her uncle and aunt had been murdered. Nate Hawthorne had worked for Johnson for a lot of years," the contact had said.

"Anything else?"

"It was hard to eavesdrop without getting caught," the contact had replied, "but I heard Johnson offer his condolences and promise that he would do everything he could to catch the killers."

Lushenska was still unsatisfied. Perhaps the woman had just called to tell Hawthorne's friends of his death. Certainly he had no reason to believe she would expose the real function of the firm her uncle and he had started.

She would be putting her own neck in a noose if she did.

He was about to tell Agca to take her home, then changed his mind. She was still Hawthorne's niece, and still filled with a need to avenge his death.

No, he decided, it would be better for everyone if she wasn't among the living. She had been a good worker, but there were many unemployed intelligence analysts begging to replace her. Perhaps he'd hire a Russian woman next time. A pretty one, of course.

"Finish the job," he said coldly.

The man on the other end grunted his acknowledgment.

No pleasantries were exchanged. Agca neither offered nor expected any. Theirs was a purely business relationship. He performed a professional service for which Lushenska paid extremely well.

"One more thing," Agca added. "I can pick up my fee today, can't I?"

The response was affirmative. The Turk looked pleased. He was getting closer to his goal. Soon he would have enough money to return to his native country and assume the new identity he had already started building, as a partner in one of the smaller opium-processing gangs.

He knew that there was a short life span for men in his line of work. Sooner or later, a client—or an enemy—would come looking for him.

He planned to change professions when he left Switzerland. Then Lushenska and the others like him could search around the world looking for traces of the missing Kammil Agca, while he found a woman to marry and start his own family.

"Time to wrap this up." He put away the cellular phone, eased the small black automatic into his hand and calmly pumped two shots into Sally Hawthorne's right eye. As blood rushed out of the shattered eye socket, the woman's head jerked back. The Turk hastily moved away from the spurting red fountain.

Agca carefully reached over and opened the front door and let the body fall onto the road, then looked down and studied the corpse. He seemed to have a sixth sense developed from years of experience that told him that there was no life left in the still form. He slammed the door shut.

Agca keyed the ignition, and the engine roared to life. It was a thirty-minute drive to where he was to meet the Russian.

All in all, a plan well executed—and very profitable. He glanced into his rearview mirror at the body blocking the entrance to the gas station. She wouldn't be found until the attendant showed up for work at six in the morning.

There would be an investigation by the local police, and the Turk suspected that they would decide that whoever had killed the woman's aunt and uncle had also killed her.

By then he would be asleep, having met with Lushenska.

And the fee for this night's work would be locked in the small, ancient safe he had built into the wall behind his bed.

There were too many thieves in Geneva to leave money just lying around.

9

Corsica

Mack Bolan eased the forty-foot powerboat into the dock at Ajaccio and jumped onto the wooden landing to tie up the vessel. Dressed in a striped T-shirt and jeans, he looked like a typical sailor—except that the motor craft he was using wasn't as sleek or modern as the others bobbing on the waters that surrounded the docks.

The soldier knew a lot about the large island. Bonaparte, the French emperor, had started his military career here. So had thugs and killers who founded the vicious criminal syndicate known as the Union Corse.

More important, the thug reputed to be the current head of the crime organization, Alexander Marius, lived on Corsica. His home was a castlelike structure halfway up the tarred road that led to the top of the tallest peak on the island.

Brognola had provided the Executioner with detailed information and maps of the island, so Bolan was prepared.

This was to be a soft probe, gathering information on Marius and the men who came for regular visits to his home.

If he needed a weapon, there was a retired American yacht broker he could contact in the nearby coastal village of Cap de Feno, who had been sent a silenced Beretta 93-R automatic and a supply of full magazines.

Bill Proger had been contacted by Hal Brognola. The retired intelligence officer was now a ship dealer and a part-time pair of ears for the United States government, reporting on political and criminal activities that might affect his country. All the lanky, elderly man knew was that he was to provide information and, if requested, the weapon to someone named Mike Belasko with no questions asked.

Bolan had studied the intel from Brognola again before he had pulled into the dock.

Corsica was the third-largest island in the Mediterranean and, despite being controlled by France, was actually closer to the Italian mainland, less than fifty miles across the sea.

At one point the island was only seven miles from the Italian island of Sardinia, to which it bore a similarity in appearance and in the attitude of its conflict-hardened inhabitants.

Bolan knew that many Corsicans still fantasized about becoming independent of France. A terrorist movement called the FLNC—the Corsican National Liberation Front—had shown its rage at being a captive of the European nation by planting bombs in the resort homes owned by French nationals, especially government and banking officials from Paris.

Corsica had a long history of being invaded. By the ancient Greeks, the Etruscans and Carthaginians, then by conquering Romans, followed by Vandals and Ostrogoths. The parade of invaders continued with the Byzantines and Franks.

By the eleventh century, the Roman Catholic Pope gave Corsica to Aragon, which was driven out by the Genoans, invading from Italy. In 1769 Genoa sold her rights to the island to France—the same year Napoleon Bonaparte was born in the island's capital, Ajaccio.

As Bolan prepared to leave the dock, he turned to find

a pair of uniformed officers waiting for him. One of them checked a page attached to his clipboard.

"You are Mr. Belasko?"

The question was asked in an unfriendly tone.

Bolan nodded.

"Your passport?"

Brognola had provided him with a passport in the Belasko identity and covered with visa stamps.

The two customs officials studied the official document carefully, examining the photograph in the passport and comparing it to the man who stood in front of them.

"We will want to examine your craft."

"Of course."

Bolan suspected he knew the source of their suspicions—Rudy Johnson. The CIA official had to have passed along a tip through his Paris staff that a mercenary who called himself Mike Belasko was coming to Corsica.

The customs men climbed aboard the craft and went below to tear apart the storage areas.

Bolan looked unconcerned. There were no weapons aboard, not even a flare gun. He had suspected that Johnson's resentment at being excluded from the protection of the President would cause him to violate the rules of secrecy that the Chief Executive had imposed on everyone at the White House meeting.

It wasn't his problem, Bolan decided. He'd pass the information on to Brognola and let him deal with it. Politics, egos and personalities were some of the reasons he severed official connection with the government.

From the information Proger had provided, the Union Corse chief ran the syndicate's businesses out of his fortress home. He had guests from all over the world visiting him, often carrying large, heavy suitcases that the former government official assumed were filled with illegally earned money.

The difficulty in arresting him was the fact that many of the island's police were on his payroll. The numerous raids on his castle by agents of the DST, the French agency responsible for stopping terrorist and criminal activities, unearthed no evidence of the criminal activities the authorities knew he had masterminded.

Proger had also related that for the past several years, representatives of some of the more notorious foreign criminal organizations had been coming to visit him on a monthly basis.

As well, a banker from Geneva, Hans Zelnick, came calling, and he was rumored to have money-laundering connections to Latin American drug lords.

The soldier's review of the situation was interrupted by the reappearance of the two customs officials. Ignoring him, they searched every inch of the deck, tearing open storage panels and reaching inside to feel for hidden weapons.

Finally, frustrated and exhausted, they turned back to Bolan.

"Do you not carry a flare gun?" one man asked.

"No, it fell overboard two nights ago. I plan to replace it here."

One of the customs men opened Bolan's passport, stamped it, then handed it back to him.

"Enjoy your stay, Mr. Belasko," he snapped.

THE RETIRED YACHT BROKER offered Bolan a drink, which he accepted.

"I don't know who you are or why you're here, Mr. Belasko." He smiled. "At my age it's probably better I don't."

The Executioner looked at the slim, aging man. Proger looked to be in his fifties.

"You're not that old," Bolan commented, setting his drink on the living-room cocktail table.

"Seventy in three weeks. But thanks for the compliment," he added gratefully. "Nice words like that will get you almost anything you want."

"Tell me about Alexander Marius."

Proger grimaced. "Scum of the worst kind. At least that's what I hear. His hoodlums control every dishonest business in Corsica, Marseilles and a lot of other French cities."

"How ambitious is he?"

"Ambitious enough to kill off the men who competed with him for the top job in the Union Corse," the yacht broker said. "How ambitious should he be for your purposes?"

Bolan took a chance and shared the rumors the man in the White House had passed along to him.

"Is he ambitious enough to hire someone to kill the President?" Bolan asked.

Proger looked surprised. "Of France?"

"Of the United States."

The elderly man emitted an involuntary whistle. "I wouldn't have thought so. At least the man on Marius's board of directors I've become friendly with didn't say anything about it. And when Phil Cambridge gets drunk, he usually brags about the big deals he's got going.

"I've seen some of the monthly visitors who fly in from around the world," he added.

"Do you know who they are?"

"Some, not all."

"Describe them."

The former CIA official searched his memory and gave the soldier a list of some of the world's elite criminal organizations.

"Does he have a blond woman who lives with him?"

"Yes. I met her once. Pretty, in a cold way. I wouldn't want her in my bed. I'd be afraid she'd act like a black widow spider. You know, have her fun, then kill me.'' He smiled. ''Of course, that would have been when I was a hell of a lot younger.''

''I guess Marius isn't worried.''

''Have you been up to his fortress yet?''

Bolan shook his head.

''He's got more servants wearing guns under their jackets than our President. If she murdered him, she wouldn't get ten feet out of that stone castle of his before one of his henchmen blew her apart.''

Bolan was still in the dark about what role Alexander Marius and his partners played in the rumored assassination.

''Anything else you heard about Marius?''

Proger became quiet, and Bolan could see his mind sifting through what he had heard.

''Nothing much. Cambridge bragged that Marius and the groups his board of directors represented were putting money into some legitimate business.'' He looked skeptical. ''I found it hard to believe, but he swore that they were buying up small-arms and ammunition companies with the backing of investors. That's how Cambridge got mixed up with him. Most of Cambridge's money has been made smuggling diamonds and gold from his mining holdings out of South Africa, without paying taxes.''

''What's that got to do with guns?''

''Phil Cambridge is a greedy pig. And among his many side investments, he owned a small company in Johannesburg that made some pretty ugly riot shotguns. When apartheid ended, orders for his weapons dried up, except for some business from street gangs. But they weren't enough to keep the company going. So he accepted the Union Corse boss's offer, and then agreed to become a member of the board of the new organization Marius was forming.''

Jackpot.

Bolan had found the connection. Now he had to find out how and when the assassination would be done—if the assassins bothered telling Marius. Based on his experience, Bolan knew that often hired professionals refused to share those details with their clients so that both of them could continue to live.

He turned to the retired CIA official. "Is Marius still in his castle?"

"I think he was planning to leave Corsica some time today."

He reached for a telephone on an end table, and dialed a number while he continued the conversation.

"I can find out fast enough. He keeps a small corporate jet at the airport just outside of Ajaccio."

Proger waited for someone to answer, then asked a question in the Corsican dialect. After a few more words, he closed the conversation and replaced the receiver.

"The fueling service at the airport received a request to fill his jet's tank. They're expecting him any minute." He smiled. "The blond woman will be traveling with him, according to the call they got."

"How do they know for sure?"

"She drinks only champagne. They were told to put a stock of chilled Bollinger on board."

"Any idea where the plane is headed?"

Proger smiled. "I'm pretty good for a retired spook, but I'm not that good. The answer is no."

Bolan stood.

"Not so fast," the yacht broker said. He got to his feet and vanished from the room. When he returned, he was carrying a small leather case, which he handed to his guest.

"I've been keeping this for you."

Bolan knew what was inside—his Beretta 93-R and several extra magazines.

10

A small Renault was parked in the bushes, peppered with bullet holes. Bolan stopped to examine it and discovered the bodies of a young couple inside, riddled with bullets.

Mack Bolan spotted an American passport on the floor of the car, near the man's body. He picked it up, opened it, and saw the smiling face of a Mr. Allan Powdermaker.

The couple had been killed slowly and painfully. The man first, the soldier assumed, because the body of the woman was nude. Someone had brutally raped her before killing her.

As familiar as he was with the sight of death, Bolan was sickened by the bodies in the car. He made some assumptions. The couple was probably on their honeymoon, judging from the newness of Powdermaker's passport, and was probably sight-seeing.

The Powdermakers had probably decided to drive to the top of the highest peak on Corsica, over nine thousand feet above sea level.

Corsica had a reputation for harboring more bandits than countries many times its size. For a moment Bolan thought some of them had been responsible for the brutal rape and slayings.

Then he searched the dead man's jacket pockets and found a wallet filled with hundred-dollar bills. With a quick glance into the car, he saw a woman's purse and the still closed luggage.

No bandits murdered the Powdermakers, he decided. Bolan stared up at the stone castle that was Alexander Marius's.

He thought he knew who the murderers were and where to find them.

A TRIO OF HOODS guarded the road that led to Marius's fortress, each armed with a 9 mm subgun.

Behind the wheel of the rented car, Bolan slipped the Beretta from its shoulder holster and tucked it into his waistband. The soft probe he had planned was turning into something much harder.

The Executioner stopped the car as one of the guards stood in the middle of the narrow road and glared at him. In French, flavored with a heavy Corsican accent, he demanded, "Where the hell do you think you are going?"

Bolan understood enough French to translate the question, but he decided to play dumb. "You speak English?"

In disgust the tough spit on the tarred road. "People who come to Corsica should at least learn our language," he snarled in broken English, then repeated his question.

"I understand there is a fabulous view of the island and the Mediterranean from the top of Mount Cinto," Bolan said, trying to sound like a tourist.

"There is," the guard snapped, "but you're not going to see it."

"Is there something wrong with the road up there?"

"No, it's because I say you're going to turn around and drive back down the road."

Bolan opened the driver's door of his rented vehicle. He could see the gunman's grip tighten around the trigger guard of the automatic weapon in his hand.

Bolan pretended to be nervous at the sight of the submachine gun. "Hey," he protested, "I just wanted to ask you a question."

The guard relaxed his grip slightly.

"So ask," the thug snarled.

Moving fast, the Executioner wrapped a well-muscled arm around the hardman's neck and turned him so that he became a shield from the other two.

"What you feel in your back is death," Bolan snapped, pushing the muzzle of the Beretta against the gunman's spinal column. "Hand the gun back to me, butt first."

Sensing the sudden tension in the guard, he added, "And do it very slowly if you want to keep living."

As if it were a delicate piece of crystal, the Corsican hood moved the arm grasping the barrel of the 9 mm MAT subgun in his left hand toward Bolan. Then he tried to fire the 9 mm MAB PA-15 semiautomatic he had yanked from his waistband.

Bolan reacted immediately, firing a pair of rounds that tore through the man's spinal column, then continued their journey through his intestines, exiting from a newly created crater in front.

The Executioner pulled his arm away and let the quivering corpse fall. Then, gripping the French subgun in his left hand, he wasted no time firing the two weapons he held at the remaining guards.

Shocked at the suddenness of the attack, the Corsicans were too slow in bringing their weapons into target acquisition. Bullets slammed into their chests, punching them backward onto the ground.

Bolan checked the corpses to ensure that they were dead, then headed out in search of other prey.

THE STOCKY MAN had taken off the servant's coat the Union Corse chief had made him wear when the directors were at the castle. Jacques saw no point looking like one of those poor slaves who worked for the rich, when his real job was to make sure his boss was always protected.

He made himself comfortable in the chair at the head of the conference table and poured himself a large glass of wine to go with the large bowl of *azimunu,* the fish stew of the island, he had placed on the antique table.

One of the men came running into the conference room, looking worried, then stopped and stared at the seated man.

"If the boss sees you there, poof, you're dead."

Jacques hauled a .357 Colt Python from its shoulder holster and slammed it onto the table. "Who's going to tell him?"

"Not me."

The head guard shoved a large spoon of the stew into his mouth, then bit off a large piece of bread from the long baguette and washed the combination down with a mouthful of the cheap, potent wine.

"Go get yourself something to eat," he ordered.

"Sure," the other man said, then started to leave.

At the doorway, he stopped and turned. "I heard shots from outside."

Jacques shook his head. "Oh, the boys are just having some fun with somebody on the road. Probably a tourist trying to get to the top of the peak."

The other guard looked unconvinced. "It sounded like a lot of shots were fired."

"So? They're just having target practice. You could use some yourself. Go outside and fire a few rounds."

Turning away from the other man, Jacques concentrated on eating his meal.

THE EXECUTIONER SCOUTED the area around the huge stone building. No one was guarding the fortress other than the three dead men he had killed on the road. And their bodies were safely hidden in a thicket of woods at the side of the Union Corse chief's headquarters.

Inside the building might be a different matter. From his

quick survey of the structure's windows, it appeared that there were at least twenty rooms, and each could hide an armed killer, just waiting to win a reward for bagging the intruder.

The soldier had searched the dead guards' pockets and found a half-dozen full magazines for their MAT submachine guns. Bolan held one of the automatic weapons in his right hand and wore a second slung across his left shoulder. The Beretta 93-R was back in its shoulder holster.

Bolan eased his way to a side door and slowly turned the handle.

Listening for a few minutes for sounds that would indicate one or more of the Union Corse gangsters were waiting in hiding, the soldier decided that, at least for the moment, the area was safe.

He entered the fortress and found himself in a hallway. Above and below him were carpeted steps, and from downstairs came the voices of two men speaking in the Corsican dialect.

The soldier shouldered the MAT subgun in his right hand and replaced it with the silenced Beretta. There was no point revealing his presence inside the Union Corse leader's house before it was necessary.

Checking the clip in the 9 mm automatic, he replaced it with a fresh, full magazine, then set the fire-selector switch to 3-shot mode.

He had no way of knowing how many of the enemy he would be facing. At least he could start with a full load of bullets.

11

Bolan used the shadows on the stairs to mask his presence. When he reached the bottom landing, he stopped and listened. There were no alarming sounds, only the noises from booted feet moving away from him.

Moving cautiously, the Executioner worked his way toward the sound of the booted feet, moving along the dimly lit corridor, hugging the wall.

As he neared a corner, shadows loomed on both walls of the hallway.

Two thickset men appeared, 9 mm MAT submachine guns cradled in their arms.

Bolan stepped away from the wall and held his 9 mm Beretta in a two-handed grip. A pair of quick bursts took the guards out of play.

A second pair of gunmen rushed to join the battle, spraying the hallway with autofire from the Russian-made AK-74s they gripped.

The Executioner flipped the fire-selector switch to full-auto and drilled the two new assailants with sustained bursts.

Dropping his AK-74, one mortally wounded hardman clutched his midsection, trying to close the suddenly created cavity in his abdomen.

His partner rushed at the Executioner, crazed by the burning lead that had shattered his right shoulder.

Turning his Kalashnikov on Bolan, the Corsican street

soldier started to unleash the carbine's awesome firepower. The soldier stopped his movement with two lead blasters that chewed into his chest, shoving him backward, dead, onto the floor.

After checking that the four were really dead, Bolan quickly scanned the area for additional men. None was in the immediate area.

Moving among the shadows, Bolan worked his way slowly through the lower level.

There was a large kitchen filled with professional-looking equipment. And next to it, a small eating area, apparently intended for the guards to use. Closets were empty, as were the storerooms.

A large food locker, intended to hold sides of beef, lamb and pork, would suit Bolan's purposes. He dragged the four bodies inside the chilled room, so no one would find them before he had completed his assault.

At the end of the corridor, he found another door, this one with a heavy lock and hasp.

A burst of well-placed rounds from the Beretta shattered the hasp. Bolan removed the spent magazine and rammed home a fresh clip, shoved the Beretta in his waistband and opened the door.

The room was a miniature armory. Cases of pistols and rifles were stacked to the ceiling, as were cases of ammunition for a variety of weapons.

A case of American rockets, obviously stolen from some military depot, was pushed into a corner, sitting next to four rocket launchers.

Bolan kept searching the room, then spotted the objective of his hunt at the far end of the storeroom.

A case of plastic explosives sat next to a mixed case of miniaturized timers and detonators. And next to them stood several cases of 40 mm incendiary and fragmentation grenades.

Glancing around the room, he found an old knapsack against a wall and filled it with eight bricks of plastique and a quantity of detonators and timers. Then he loaded a number of both types of grenades into the bag.

Shouldering the knapsack, the Executioner turned to leave, then heard the sound of footsteps walking toward the storeroom door.

A voice shouted out, "Michel, what the hell are you doing in the armory? We took inventory yesterday."

Bolan pressed his back to the wall next to the open door.

A tall, stout, balding man stepped inside the door and looked around. "Michel?"

Wrapping a hard-muscled arm around the guard's neck, Bolan squeezed against the thug's throat.

The bald man struggled to get free, kicking backward in an attempt to trip his assailant.

Reaching up with his other hand, the Executioner pressed the palm firmly against the guard's chin, then twisted the men's head until he heard the soft snapping of bones. Slowly the Corsican's life fled his limp body, until he slumped like a huge rag doll.

Bolan lowered the body to the ground, then dragged it behind a stack of cases.

Closing the door behind him, the soldier knew it was time to check the rest of the fortress.

BOLAN FOUND a small office on the lower level. Locked metal file cabinets lined one wall.

He searched the desk drawer and found a ring filled with keys that fit the locks.

The first cabinet seemed to have files on individuals, most likely Marius's men. Bolan was sure that the French authorities knew all—or most—of them.

He went to the second file cabinet. The drawers were filled with financial records, nothing very unusual. The various items had code names, except for one folder, which bore the name Hans Zelnick.

Scanning the contents, Bolan found Swiss bank records and decided to save them. Emptying the folder, he shoved the pages into the knapsack he'd confiscated.

The third and fourth cabinets contained more Union Corse records, with code words replacing the names of their various activities. Bolan was sure the French national police—the DST—already had files on them.

The top drawer of the final cabinet was labeled Armament, in French.

The soldier unlocked the cabinet and scanned the titles on the folders. They were financial records for more than a dozen different companies located in eleven countries, and a list of investors, again disguised by code words.

This was some of the information he had been seeking. The folders went into the canvas knapsack.

Lists of customers for each of the companies dominated the rest of the cabinet. Grabbing the folders that dealt with doing business with crime cartels and terrorist groups, Bolan knelt and opened the bottom drawer.

The first folder, labeled Contractors, again in French, caught his eye.

Instinctively he knew that this was the most important of all the information in the filing cabinets.

Flipping through the pages, Bolan spotted records of contacts with some group in Geneva, Switzerland. The name was in code, but the Executioner was certain he knew their true identity.

This was the connection.

He was positive Marius headed the group who wanted the President of the United States murdered.

As he shoved the folders into his knapsack, Bolan fit the various pieces of the puzzle together.

Marius and his group had acquired arms manufacturers,

hoping to make a killing by selling weapons to traditionally hostile sides. The effective campaign by the American government, urging a reduction in disputes that could only be settled by the use of killing machines, had put the syndicate's future in serious jeopardy.

Most businesses faced with the same dilemma would search for a way to manufacture something other than guns or ammo, but not a criminal like the head of the Union Corse.

Or his crime-syndicate partners.

They were determined to stay in the same business, even if it meant feeding enemies the means to murder millions of innocent women and children.

Bolan was more determined than ever to see them fail.

His thoughts were interrupted by the harsh voice behind him, snarling in French, "Who the hell are you?"

Bolan made an instant decision. It was kill or be killed, nothing less, nothing more.

Unleathering the Beretta 93-R, he knew he didn't have enough time to take careful aim. Instead, he tried to use the voice as a guide to where his target was standing, or had been standing when he spoke.

A little to his right, Bolan decided.

He then dived to his left as a stream of heated lead tore into the file cabinet that had been behind him.

Twisting his body, the Executioner pushed himself up on his elbows and hosed the armed man with a burst of lead.

Stunned at the suddenness of the response, the enemy gunner stared in disbelief at Bolan, then fell to the floor, face forward, the growing pool of blood pouring from his ruined abdomen.

The Executioner hoisted the heavy knapsack onto a shoulder. There was one more thing he had to do before he contacted Brognola and asked for a swift way to get the files to him.

Sitting at the desk, he reloaded the Beretta and holstered it. Then, digging through the bag, he hauled out the bricks of plastique and primed each with a timer and detonator.

The soldier wasn't sure if there was anyone else still alive in the stone building. But he was certain they would be dead after he planted the plastique and its awesome power was unleashed.

As he approached the stairs, Beretta now in hand, the Executioner spotted a shadow moving at the top of the stairs and waited until he could verify that what he was seeing was an armed enemy.

When the gunner revealed himself, the Executioner squeezed off a pair of shots. The hardman groaned and dropped his weapon. He had made the mistake of sticking his head out from behind the corner to see who had been firing shots.

Both shots had drilled into the point of the man's neck where the head and spine met. A shower of blood spurted out of the gaping wound as he slumped across the steps.

Another man, his right hand loaded with dinner dishes, walked around the corner.

He stared at the weapon in the Executioner's hand and threw the dishes at him.

Then he reached inside his waistband for the .357 Colt Python secreted there.

Calmly Bolan let his finger glide back on the trigger and released a trio of 9 mm parabellum rounds.

The dish carrier dropped the weapon in his hand and started to speak. "I was only going to the kitchen to…"

The bullets had shattered the brain cortex, and he died before he could finish his explanation.

A bulky gunman stared at the bodies on the stairs and raced back up them. Bolan waited patiently, and the gunman reappeared, a TEC-9 subgun in his hands.

He washed the bottom of the stairs with lead, but Bolan

had already moved around the corner. The sound of metal clinking on metal echoed loudly.

The Executioner knew the Corsican's gun was empty. He showed himself again. It was time to finish this phase of the battle.

The Union Corse killer snapped a fresh magazine into his autoweapon, and sprayed a burst across the bottom of the staircase. "Die, you son of a bitch," he yelled in French.

A burst of 9 mm rounds from Bolan's Beretta tore holes into the street soldier's chest, traveling through his sternum and out his back.

The Executioner watched as the hardman tumbled to the floor. Looking down at him, the Executioner said his own form of last rites.

"You first."

CAREFULLY HE PLANTED the plastic explosives strategically around the fortress. The Union Corse would have to find a new headquarters in less than a half hour. When he finished the job, Bolan returned to his vehicle and, racing down the Mount Cinto road, decided to use the retired Agency man's phone to place a security call to Brognola.

Then it would be time to leave the island and head for his next destination.

As he reached the juncture in the mountain road and turned onto the narrow two-lane coastal highway, the first of the explosions erupted. A torrent of ancient stones and bricks studded the sky above the fortress with a shower of shattered building material.

The arms cache went next. Smashing their way through lower-level windows and doors, rockets, grenades and ammunition filled the air with a blinding shower of chemical light.

Flames climbed skyward through the openings that had once been covered with tiles and stones.

Marius's castle was destroyed, even if his empire wasn't. At least not yet.

12

The French Alps

Margaritta Schindler sat alone in first class and dozed as the half-empty high-speed train left the Geneva station and started its forty-three-mile run to the French Alps village of Megeve. From there a helicopter would fly her to the resort village of Courchevel, located high in the Alps at the end of a steep, narrow alpine road that dead-ended in the center of the tiny community.

As Schindler knew, there was more than one resort named Courchevel. Each had its elevation in meters listed after its name. Courchevel 1850, for example, was 1850 meters above sea level.

From the village square, a waiting Volkswagen van, fitted with oversize tires to handle the roads that were icy year-round, would drive her to the tiny Hotel Everest, which sat at the upper reaches of the winter resort. Marius had chosen it because it offered total privacy from snoopers and because the Union Corse owned it.

His personal army of Corsican street soldiers would take care of any unwelcome visitors who tried to approach the hotel.

It had been a long and difficult trip from Corsica to Geneva.

THE JOURNEY HAD STARTED the day before when the Union Corse chief and Schindler left the island in his private jet.

As the modified Mystère-Falcon 20F had climbed into the clear skies above Corsica, she had seen Marius studying her, then smile as his devoted servant, Germain, popped the cork on a bottle of champagne. The soft hum of the General Electric engines filled the cabin with a gentle vibration that relaxed the passengers in its luxurious interior.

Marius watched the vintage bubbles glisten in Schindler's glass, then became serious.

"Make the deal with the Russian," he said coldly.

"I thought you wanted to explore other possibilities," she countered. "If you remember my report, the Caribbean contract ended with both assassins getting themselves killed."

"If you are nervous, I can always send Germain," he commented.

"I thought you'd want me to observe at least one more assignment, given how badly they bungled the last one. Not even the Baader-Meinhof Gang wasted lives so readily."

"Who cares?" The Union Corse chief seemed indifferent. "What matters is that they completed their assignment. The president-elect of the country is dead."

Schindler couldn't understand why Marius was pushing so hard to use an outside contractor when he had her.

"Time is running out," the Corsican stated. "I'll drop you in Geneva. The banker will meet you at the Russian's office. He'll have a suitcase with half of their fee."

She looked annoyed.

"Something bothering you?"

She swallowed the rest of the champagne in the glass. "It's absurd bringing in outsiders when I am available."

"You're good, my dear," the stocky man admitted, "but I will use you on this assignment only as a last resort."

His tone became icy.

"So don't bring the subject up again."

Schindler shrugged. She had survived a long time and knew when to stop arguing.

"Meantime," Marius said, sounding more pleasant, "finish your business in Geneva quickly and come to Courchevel. I will be lonely without you."

"You'll be tied up in meetings day and night," she said, pouting.

"So will you."

He glanced down at a small leather bag. "I'm bringing your favorite guns just in case somebody steps out of line."

At least she would be involved in the assassination, she decided as she leaned her head back against the upholstered seat.

NOW SHE WAS meeting Marius. The man was an animal in bed, no sophistication or finesse. She knew his lovemaking techniques would leave her feeling like she had been used.

She was too exhausted to pretend she enjoyed it, but it didn't matter. The crime-syndicate head would be too busy satisfying himself to notice.

She would have to do something about the man, but this wasn't the time. Not yet. Only after she found something else that would satisfy her need for money and properly use her skills.

For killing.

But as tired as she was, she was flattered at the glances of interest from the handful of male passengers aboard the train. It always happened, although few of them ever got the courage to actually approach her.

Margaritta Schindler knew she was attractive, even pretty, when she found that useful. She had worked hard at being beautiful. At thirty-six, she looked as good, if not better, than she did at twenty.

The previous night her appearance was important to her.

She had tried to interest Lushenska into spending the night with her. But the former KGB general ignored her overtures.

So she settled on Hans Zelnick. After their meeting with the Russian, she had invited the Swiss banker to join her for a late-night drink in her hotel suite.

She had enjoyed watching him try to be charming as she led him step by step through her seduction routine. He had been dull in bed, but now she owned him, as she had hoped to own the Russian.

She knew Zelnick wanted to have her again and was terrified that either Marius or his overweight wife would find out about them.

But at the moment, dressed in a pair of wrinkled jeans and matching wool-lined jacket, she didn't care what she looked like. That could wait until she would be required to put on the costume that made her look attractive to Marius.

She had been traveling for almost two hours, with little sleep the night before. The formfitting jeans she'd worn since she'd started the journey were cutting into her. The thin Western-style shirt she was wearing was starting to acquire the odor of her perspiration. She was starting to feel fatigue dueling with that part of her that warned her to stay awake and alert.

The fatigue was beginning to win.

What she needed was a bath, some sleep and fresh clothes. She would have to stop in a bathroom when they arrived in Megeve and put on more-feminine clothes.

She sat up quickly and forced herself to stare out the window at the mountain-studded world outside. Mountain followed mountain in a monotonous parade, lulling her brain into a semiconscious condition again.

There was too much to get done before she could allow herself to rest. She forced herself to review her meeting with the Russian.

"I UNDERSTAND the orders. They are very explicit," the stocky, bald man growled, glaring first at the Swiss banker who had accompanied Schindler to the meeting and then at her. "Our responsibility is to make sure the American President is dead. Then to make sure that there is no way your organization is linked to the assassination."

She remembered the expression on his face when she interrupted.

"And your third is to keep your eyes and ears open for any useful information the Americans might reveal," she added briskly.

"Of course."

Lushenska stood and came out from behind his desk so that he was close to her when he offered her advice. "Let us handle the assignment. I know you have a reputation in these kinds of matters, but we are the experts."

She lowered her gaze and muttered, "Understood."

Both she and the Russian knew she resented Marius's hiring them for an assignment she had felt she could handle without assistance. The fury she felt at being pushed aside by the Corsican burned in the deepest parts of her soul and bubbled like a caldron of stinking poison. Marius would die at her hand, but only when the time was right.

WHEN BOLAN contacted Brognola to report on the destruction of Marius's castle and the documents, the big Fed had told him to give them to Proger, who had a secure fax machine. He went on to say that new information had apparently come to light.

A meet was set for later that night in a café in Paris. Mack Bolan didn't like the idea of exposing the purpose of the mission to anyone, especially CIA agents.

Brognola had told him the two field men had gotten some information on who had been hired to handle the assassination.

Bolan was puzzled. "Why didn't they send the info by secure fax?"

"You know how the CIA is. Everyone who works for them is a ham actor at heart. If they can't have their moment of stardom, they won't play," Brognola commented. "Meet with them, but don't turn your back on them. The White House orders may be to treat Mike Belasko with kid gloves, but I can't guarantee the message got down to the street level. Or that the pair you're meeting will pay any attention to it."

Paris

BOLAN ARRIVED at Orly Airport midafternoon. His bags would arrive an hour later on an American-government jet flying diplomatic supplies to the embassy in Paris.

The first of the two bags he expected to be delivered held his arsenal, a pair of mini-Uzi submachine guns, a silenced 9 mm Beretta 93-R, a .44 Magnum Desert Eagle and an Applegate-Fairbairn combat knife housed in a firm sheath.

An assortment of ammo for the weapons was packed in the bag, as were a dozen compact plastic explosives fitted with miniaturized triggers and timers and an array of 40 mm incendiary and fragmentation grenades that could be delivered from an M-203 grenade launcher.

The second canvas bag contained money he had acquired from the criminal syndicates he had battled on previous missions.

The Executioner waited for the plane to arrive, then picked up his bags and loaded them into the Peugeot sedan he had rented at the airport.

The safehouse was a small, two-story brick building in the Tenth Arrondissement. Surrounded by porn houses and second-run movie theaters, the tiny structure was largely ignored by men rushing to see the newest in nudity, or to see Hollywood's latest film export.

Bolan had parked the rented car in the alley behind the safehouse, then opened the carryall bag and stripped his weapons. He carefully cleaned each part. It was important that none of them jammed because of some dirt or residual gunpowder.

He had lots of time. The appointment was for midnight.

It was eleven-thirty when Bolan left the safehouse Brognola had lined up for him and got into the rented vehicle. The trip to the café would take only minutes, but the Executioner planned to recon the area before the sitdown took place.

THE ALL-NIGHT CAFÉ where Bolan was supposed to meet the pair of field agents was in Les Halles, the ancient food-wholesale district of Paris. Where once buckets of garlic-scented snails and bowls of onion soup were standard fare, cups of thick, bitter coffee and pastries were now the passion of workers and visitors who wandered through the area.

Many ended their all-night carousing with a bowl of onion soup at Au Pied de Cochon or at Au Chien Qui Fume, the last two famous remnants of the time when wholesale butchers cut carcasses into restaurant or grocery-store cuts, and vegetable dealers sold the latest in domestic or imported crops.

But unlike in its heyday, the crowds of tourists and partying locals vanished from the Rue de Turbigo and the tiny streets that spread from it around midnight.

Two men, dressed in jeans and sweaters, sat huddled over their coffee cups.

One of them checked his wristwatch. "Where is this Belasko?"

"He'll be here soon enough," his companion replied, looking around the nearly empty food shop.

"I didn't see the Apache when I parked my car."

Both men knew the nickname applied to Algerians, French and Arab, who lived in the slum districts of Paris and made their living outside of the law.

"Typical Algerian. He's hiding someplace outside so he can ambush Belasko instead of being straight up and facing him directly."

"Anybody else waiting out there?"

"He brought one or two other freelancers with him. Naturally he's going to charge us for two."

"Good. From what I was told, Belasko is more than just a handful."

The second man smiled. "So is the Apache and his pals."

The agents had been ordered by Langley to meet with the visitor. Then the caller added, "Just make sure he doesn't leave the area alive. And I don't want any of our people directly involved."

Usually the field agents would have demanded the assignment be put in writing, but not from someone so high up on the CIA ladder, not when the caller was Rudy Johnson, deputy director of operations.

13

Something felt wrong. Bolan couldn't give the uneasy feelings a name or explanation, but every instinct warned him he was being set up by the men he was supposed to meet.

He parked the Peugeot on a side street and checked his armament. The Beretta was leathered under his jacket, and the Desert Eagle rode his right hip. His combat knife was strapped to his left forearm.

Under his jacket, hanging from a soft leather sling, was a Mini-Uzi submachine gun, ready to be tilted up to deliver its thirty rounds of death.

Slipping magazines for the three weapons into his jacket pockets, the Executioner looked inside the canvas bag on the floor and decided to clip an M-40 delay fragmentation grenade to his belt.

Now he was ready for anything.

Opening the door of the sedan, he studied the nearby darkened doorways. No one seemed to be hiding in any of them, but Bolan knew a trained assassin could make his presence almost invisible.

He moved slowly to the corner. There, a hundred yards away, was the coffee shop, brightly lit.

He could see the two men waiting inside, CIA field agents, trying to look like locals. Their crew cuts exposed their American origins.

Bolan heard a sound behind him, a soft, whispering noise. Rubber-soled shoes on pavement?

The soldier tilted the silenced Uzi so its stubby snout poked through the front of his jacket, then he pivoted quickly.

A swarthy man was moving rapidly in his direction, and Bolan paused momentarily to confirm that the man was holding a suppressed gun.

Once Bolan confirmed that the man was an enemy, he fired a pair of whispering rounds at the would-be assassin, shattering his breastbone and tearing open the thin jacket of tissue that held his liver in place.

The attacker tried to raise his composite-framed weapon, then let it slide from his suddenly limp hand.

For a brief moment the swarthy man wavered, trying to keep himself on his feet, then gave up and wilted to the ground.

Two men moved into the open from their doorway hide-outs, both carrying automatic subguns. One held an Italian-made 9 mm SOCIMI Type 821 submachine gun in his large, callused hands. The other kept the 9 mm Ingram MAC-10 out in front of him.

Briefly glancing at each other, the pair of gunners turned and raised their rapid-fire weapons.

Bolan spun out of the path of the blazing bullets, then pivoted back to face the gunners.

A trio of 9 mm rounds slammed into the nearer attacker, spinning him before he collapsed to the ground in a lifeless heap.

The second gunner dived into a doorway and pressed his frame against the metal entrance. Poking his head out from cover, the hardman unleashed a continuous stream of lead at where the Executioner had been standing.

The problem was that Bolan was no longer there.

He had raced behind a panel truck parked at the curb and waited for the second shooter to empty his weapon.

The sound of metal clicking on metal was the signal.

As the hired gunman panicked and tried to force a fresh magazine into his weapon, the Executioner showed himself.

"Drop it," he shouted, pointing his Uzi at his attackers.

The thug ignored the order and finally forced the fresh clip into the MAC-10.

Bolan fired a burst that shattered the face and neck of the terrified street killer. Blood spurted like a red fountain from the ruptured carotid artery, and like a puppet with its strings cut, the dead gunman collapsed to the sidewalk.

The two men in the coffee shop rushed outside, jerking .45 Colt Government pistols from waistband holsters on the run.

Staring briefly at the three corpses, the CIA agents took the two-hand Weaver's stance they'd learned on the government range and kicked off the safeties on their pistols.

Bolan didn't waste time. These men had to be the pair he was supposed to meet. While the Executioner would never shoot a policeman doing his job, taking out rogue CIA agents who were trying to kill him was a different matter.

Startled by Bolan as he rushed toward them, the pair hesitated, giving the Executioner an edge. He triggered the Uzi, hosing the men with sustained bursts that drove them to the ground.

Quickly he searched their jackets. Both carried leather identification cases that verified they worked for the Central Intelligence Agency.

One of them had a folded piece of paper in his wallet. Neatly typed was the physical description of Michael Belasko and notes that his death had to look like an attack by street thugs, looking to kill and rob a tourist.

The sounds of a police car coming closer wailed a warning.

It was time for the Executioner to retreat and to call Brognola.

AFTER WAITING for the cutouts to run through the sequence that would finally connect him to Hal Brognola's private line at the Department of Justice in Washington, D.C., Bolan told him about the assassination attempts.

"I just heard about it," the big Fed growled. "My screwup, Striker. I'm sorry."

"The agents went for their guns, so I had to take them out. But I don't get it. Who was paying the bills?"

"The CIA, as it turns out."

Bolan was surprised. He had sat in the Oval Office and heard the Man order the CIA rep to keep his hands off.

"Well, you took out the cowboys, and the President just canned the foreman of the ranch," Brognola explained.

"You mean Johnson set this up?"

"That's how the Man and I read it."

"Why? Was somebody paying him off?"

"Only his ego. The President gave him twenty-four hours to get his stuff together, sign up for the pension fund and vanish for good."

"Maybe somebody ought to do an exit interview with him and find out what he knows that he hasn't told anybody."

"Good idea. I'll get on it right away."

Bolan changed the subject. "What's the next move?"

"Forget asking the CIA for information. This time you're totally on your own."

Bolan shook his head, knowing Brognola couldn't see the gesture. "I guess that's better than having to walk around with eyes in back of your head."

As usual, the soldier knew he'd have to depend on his own contacts and instincts to complete the mission.

He remembered one: Henri Fabray, former hot shot for the DSGE, the French Intelligence service.

If he was still alive.

In Fabray's line of work, that was an accomplishment—or a miracle.

14

The small man who sat across the table from Bolan was too busy with the breakfast meal in front of him to bother talking.

Bolan studied Fabray, noting that the Frenchman had changed. He was stouter—the price of living well—and looked much older. What had once been a thick crown of black hair was now colored steel gray.

The one thing Fabray hadn't lost was the alert look in his eyes.

Finally the Frenchman ordered another cup of coffee.

"With milk," he told the waiter. "And bring that damned artificial sugar with you."

A ghost of a smile touched Bolan's lips. Even France was becoming diet conscious.

Fabray saw the expression on the soldier's face and patted the paunch around his waist. "The price of living too well for too long," he explained. Then his voice became somber. "The Paris police found four bodies in the Les Halles district last night."

"Really?"

"Two of them were CIA. The other two were contract French-Algerian killers."

"Shame."

"I thought you'd like to know," Fabray replied. Then, studying the bored expression on Bolan's face, he gave up trying to get any information from the American.

The Executioner decided to change the subject. "When was the last time you were out in the field, Henri?"

Fabray was one of the best intelligence agents his country had ever employed—fast, ruthless, an expert with a variety of weapons, and he had an instinct for survival that rivaled Bolan's.

The Frenchman leaned over and rapped a fist on his left leg, then pulled up his pant leg and exposed the prothesis that was replacing his missing leg. Smiling at Bolan's surprised expression, he pulled down his pant leg and sat up again.

"When I lost this." He shrugged. "The risks one takes in this business. An encounter with a group of ungrateful terrorists in Beirut two years ago. They died but took my left leg with them."

Bolan had fought alongside the Frenchman, and he knew it wasn't as simple as Fabray was making it sound.

"So you're out of the DSGE."

"In a way. They took me out of the field and made me a section head. Now I sit all day and read dull reports from dull people from around the world. I read something several years ago that said my old friend, Mack Bolan, was dead. Killed in a shoot-out. A shame. Such a dedicated man."

He studied the Executioner's face.

"The plastic surgeon didn't do a bad job." He leaned closer and stared at Bolan's face, then shrugged. "But those eyes might betray your true identity one day."

Bolan knew there were some things the surgeon couldn't alter, such as the cold, piercing stare from his icy blue eyes.

"What do you call yourself these days?"

"'Mike Belasko' will do for now."

Fabray tilted his head to stare at the ceiling. "So, tell me, why are you willing to buy a fat old former field agent a meal?"

Bolan had hoped to get some information on who might

be behind the rumored assassination plot against the President. He said so.

"A lot of people would like to see him dead. I suspect members of the other political party in your country wouldn't mind attending his funeral if it meant one of their own would be elected to replace him."

The soldier remembered that the Frenchman liked to milk a conversation for every bit of drama. He controlled his impatience and let Fabray ramble.

"Of course, there are those in the Middle East who would pay handsomely to have him killed, especially those who regard America as the Great Satan."

Bolan's gut instinct told him those behind the rumored plot had a more sinister purpose than just furthering their religious cause.

Out of left field, Fabray asked a question. "When was the last time you were in Lebanon?"

Bolan shrugged. "Not so long ago. A few months."

"You should go back. The beaches are so magnificent, and the skiing in the mountains has gotten so much better." He paused, then added, "I was there two weeks ago."

Bolan wondered why the Frenchman brought up his visit to Beirut.

"I ran into some old acquaintances in the casinos in Beirut while I was there," Fabray added. "You may remember one of them. Saloman Moussad."

The Executioner did. Moussad ran a small bank in the capital city of Lebanon, but his depositors were mostly representatives of the various Muslim and Christian terrorist gangs who operated out of the war-torn country.

Bolan knew it would do no good to push the man facing him. The DSGE official would share information only if it served his country's cause.

"What's he up to these days?"

"Very fat. And very rich." Fabray smiled. "He also

drinks too much, which is not a wise thing for a Muslim to do in public."

The soldier knew Moussad was a con man. "He must have found a new group of suckers."

"He claims he found a gold mine." Fabray shrugged. "Not literally, but he was boasting that his investors would be coming into a great deal of money very shortly."

"What's the scheme?"

"It turns out Moussad is on the board of directors of a combine of small-munitions manufacturers."

"With our President preaching disarmament and winning our allies to his point of view, I would think making guns and ammo is a risky investment," Bolan said casually.

"So would I, my old friend. But not Moussad. He boasted that the board has invited all the managers to a meeting to urge them to double or triple their production."

Bolan leaned forward. "What does he know that we don't know?"

"Perhaps the combine has found a way to silence the advocates of peaceful solutions to problems with their neighbors," Fabray replied.

"Any idea where and when the meeting is taking place?"

"No," the Frenchman admitted, "but I may know someone who does."

He studied the Executioner's face. "My knowledge depends on your willingness to let me accompany you when you talk to this man."

Bolan knew that the Frenchman understood that he liked to work alone. The Executioner wanted no responsibility for another human being's life.

"Done."

Fabray grinned. "It will be good to get a taste of movement again. A welcome relief from those stacks of bureaucratic trash I am forced to read every day.

"The man I refer to sold the small-arms plant he owned just outside of Mulhouse to a foreign investment group. He now runs the business for them. He manufacturs handguns and a small line of combat shotguns. Perhaps he would be willing to share whatever information he has with us. Out of loyalty to France, of course."

Bolan completed the thought that had run through both of their minds. "Or out of a fear of death."

Fabray nodded. "Exactly."

As the Eurocopter BO 105 CBS headed for the French-German-Swiss border city of Mulhouse, Bolan sat on the bench seat in the rear of the craft and spent the time stripping and cleaning the weapons in his canvas carryall.

Fabray smiled as he watched the soldier break down the weapons, then run swabs of solvent through them. As Bolan reassembled the weapons, the Frenchman hauled out the 9 mm MAB PA-15 he wore in a shoulder holster under his jacket, released the 15-round magazine and pressed the muzzle to his eye. Then he snapped the clip back into the pistol.

"You always were the careful one," Fabray commented as Bolan reloaded the weapons and placed them back into the canvas bag.

"I'm still alive."

The DSGE official shook his head. "A lot of artillery to carry just to interview a man."

"In case he decides to take exception to the questions with one of his products," Bolan replied.

"Good point."

Fabray reached under his seat and pulled out a long leather bag. After he unzipped it, he took out the 9 mm MAT-49 submachine gun stored inside.

"I had the same thought," he added with a thin smile.

The Eurocopter raced eastward toward the Voges Mountains at 129 knots, powered by a pair of Allison 250-C20B turboshafts.

Fabray had used his position to commandeer the aircraft from the French police, but brought his own DSGE crew to operate the swift transport.

"Interesting place, this Mulhouse," the French Intelligence official commented. "Much of it still looks like it must have in medieval times."

"One thing's sure. It's not downtown Los Angeles," Bolan responded.

The Frenchman smiled. "True. Even with the area bouncing back and forth between the Germans and us, nothing much has changed here, except for the introduction of some new manufacturing businesses."

He decided to give Bolan a brief lesson on the confused international status of Mulhouse.

"The Germans call the city Mulhausen. It still straddles France and Germany, and because it sits between the French Voges and the German Black Forest, the people speak both German and French."

He added, patting his protruding stomach, "And if we finish our business quickly, perhaps we can borrow a police car and drive a short distance on the E9 to Switzerland, and have dinner in Basel."

Dinner was the last thing on Bolan's mind. He had to get intel on the rumored assassination. Who had ordered it, and why? Who would be doing it? And where? He had a lot of questions to which he now had only vague, possible answers.

He changed the subject. "How soon do we get into Mulhouse?"

Fabray checked his wristwatch. "Twenty-five minutes. A police car will be waiting at the small airport."

15

Mulhouse, France

Werner LaFontaine was obviously uncomfortable as he escorted his two visitors into his small office. The general manager of the small munitions company tried to control his shaking hands as he sat down behind his paper-crowded desk.

"You said it was a government matter," he said, looking at Henri Fabray. "Is something wrong?"

The French official shook his head. "No, of course not. There are some things about your business that puzzle me, but I am sure you can clear up any confusion in a few minutes."

The assurance hadn't calmed the factory manager.

"Do you know a man named Saloman Moussad?"

LaFontaine's Adam's apple bobbed up and down as he tried to swallow his fears.

"Moussad?" He pretended to think. "I'm not sure. But we get so many buyers each year."

"Mr. Moussad claims that he is a member of the board of directors who bought your company," Fabray said coldly.

The factory owner forced a smile on his face. "Oh, that Moussad." He tried to sound glib. "The reason the name wasn't familiar is that I only met him once, when the papers were signed to buy my company."

Fabray nodded, then stated in a harsh tone, "Mr. Moussad claims he has met you on a number of occasions. That he has even visited your factory."

The nervousness returned. "Is there something wrong?"

"Your lack of candor."

A door behind them opened. As LaFontaine looked past his two visitors, Bolan and Fabray turned to see who had entered.

The man was large, almost brutish. His face was covered with faint scars, as if he had once been a professional prizefighter and still bore the marks of the ring.

He stood in the doorway, glaring at the two men.

"This is Alain Chadel, my comanager," La Fontaine stated.

Bolan studied the man. Under the loose work jacket he wore, the soldier saw the faint outline of a shoulder-holstered weapon.

"Now that both of you are here," Bolan said, taking over the conversation, "we want to know why you have increased your production to full capacity."

"That's how we make money," LaFontaine replied quickly. "By manufacturing as much as we can." He looked at the man in work clothes. "Isn't that right, Alain?"

Alain Chadel nodded.

"I would like to see a list of the customers who have ordered more than a dozen weapons," the DSGE official stated.

"It will take me some time to get such a list assembled," LaFontaine complained. "And we are so busy." He looked at Chadel. "Isn't that right, Alain?"

The larger man nodded again.

"The government is asking for the list." Fabray shrugged. "Of course, we can shut you down until such a list is produced."

"Please, no. I am meeting with the board tomorrow to review our progress. I simply can't take the time to get you a list."

"Where are you meeting?"

"I am supposed—" LaFontaine began, then caught himself and stared at the man he had called his comanager, panic in his expression.

"We can get you the list after we get back from the meeting," Chadel growled.

"I suggest you start working on it now. There is a restaurant whose cuisine I've wanted to sample for many years. We will be back after lunch to get your list," Fabray snapped.

Then he gestured to Bolan that they leave.

BOLAN COULD SENSE Fabray's disapproval as he cut into the steak he'd ordered.

"You may be many things, my friend, but you are not a connoisseur of fine food."

As Bolan watched Fabray tear into the stuffed quail, he asked a question. "Do you think they'll have a list ready for us?"

"No."

"Neither do I."

"What do you think they will have?"

Bolan patted the holster under his loose-fitting jacket. "A reception committee."

Fabray looked down at the soft leather case sitting on the carpeted floor near him. "So do I. So let us enjoy a fine meal before we enjoy a good fight."

To the death, Bolan added silently.

BOTH BOLAN AND FABRAY sensed that something had changed since they had left the factory. As they walked to the front door, they looked at each other, hoping the other had the answer.

"It's really quiet."

The Frenchman nodded. "As if nobody were inside."

Earlier the plant had been filled with men and women, working at precision tools and grinders.

Bolan took a guess. "Lunch hour?"

"Hardly. It is after two in the afternoon. No Frenchman—or woman—could wait until such an hour to eat. It goes against the nature."

"Then we might be in for a surprise." Bolan looked down at Fabray's leg. "Are you ready for it."

"Have you seen me limp?"

Bolan hadn't, and he shook his head.

"Then not only am I ready, I am anxious for something to begin."

The Executioner moved ahead of Fabray and peered through the thick window set into the heavy metal door.

"Doesn't look like there's anybody inside. Wait here. I'll try to look through the other windows."

Dirt prevented a clear view of the interior, but Bolan could make out the machines. Nobody was working at them. It was as if everybody inside had vanished from the face of the earth.

He returned to the front door. "They're all gone. At least the workers are," he announced.

"What now?"

"We check inside."

Bolan tried to turn the knob on the front door. It was locked. He gestured for Fabray to stand back, then fired a burst from the Uzi at the lock.

The metal shattered under the impact.

"Now we can go inside, " Bolan said, replacing the magazine.

"MAYBE WE SHOULD hide behind some of the bigger machines," one of the three men crouching behind a row of grinders whispered.

"The chief said to stay here," the second man replied. "Besides, the three are behind them."

"What about the chief?"

"He and the little guy left for the meeting in Courchevel. He said to tell everybody there'll be a nice bonus when he gets back."

"When do we start firing?" the third gunman asked.

"The moment the two men are in the open area inside the front door, of course. The chief wants this over as soon as possible. He and the little stooge who pretends to be boss have to leave in the morning for the meeting."

Each man checked his weapon. The 9 mm Heckler & Koch MP-5 SD-3 silenced submachine guns were fitted with a 30-round magazine.

Then they watched as the doorknob turned.

"FOLLOW MY LEAD," Bolan whispered.

He pushed the door open with a foot, then leaned back.

A shower of lead from inside sprayed around and through the opening.

The Executioner fell to his stomach, waited until the volley ended, then inched his way inside the building, pushing the Uzi subgun in front of him.

He could hear the sound of metal rubbing metal as the assailants changed magazines. He lowered his head to the stone floor and waited until a second wave of death-seekers tore into the street outside the stone industrial building.

Bolan could sense Henri Fabray lying next to him. The stout Frenchman turned his head.

"What next?" he whispered.

"We wait until I signal that we make our move." He turned his head slightly so that Fabray could hear him.

"When I do rush into the building, dump lead in front of you at the nearest row of machines, then find a place to hide and reload."

"Understood."

Finally the second lead shower ceased.

"Now," Bolan whispered, and jumped to his feet.

Running a broken path like a halfback heading for the goal, Bolan emptied his Uzi in the direction of the gunners.

He heard the grunt of a man hit by the Uzi rounds, then rolled at a right angle from where he'd entered, turning on his stomach to unleash a hellstorm of death at whoever was using the row of grinders as shields.

Behind him he could hear the scraping of Fabray's metal prothesis as the Frenchman tried to keep up with him.

A dark figure rose from behind a workbench, cursing. Before the Executioner could take him out, he heard Fabray's MAT spout a short burst.

The hardman spun, then fell backward and crashed into one of the smaller machines.

A second gunner, obviously wounded from the way he dragged his right leg, tried to escape through the open front door. There was no time for the Executioner to take careful aim. He loosed a pair of rounds at the limping thug.

Screaming foul threats, the would-be killer turned and tried to charge Bolan. A second pair of hollow rounds ended his charge. He crashed into a workbench, scattering metal parts to the floor. Then, with a soft, final gasp, the corpse fell to the stone floor and was suddenly still.

The soldier spun out of the way of a brief burst of gunfire. Behind him he heard the French Intelligence agent mutter a curse.

As he turned, he saw Fabray climb to his feet and angrily hose the area in front of him with a full load from the MAT's magazine, then fall to his knees.

Bolan crawled to him. "You okay?"

"That bastard," Fabray snarled. "One of his shots tore into my leg."

Bolan reached over to pull up the Frenchman's pant leg and examine the wound.

"Not that one," he snapped. "My artificial one."

Bolan cocked an eyebrow.

"Do you know how long it took for me to get the government to agree to have one made?"

"You stay here and I'll take care of the rest of them," the soldier suggested.

Before the Frenchman could reply, the shadow of a wide figure popped up from behind a precision machine and scattered lead from his submachine gun in a wide sweep of the room.

"Stay down," Bolan ordered while he watched the paunchy man change magazines.

Instead, Fabray rammed home a fresh clip, pulled himself erect and unloaded a half-dozen rounds at where the shadow had appeared. The heavy lead loads slammed against the wall behind the machines, then wildly took flight in different directions.

The death screams from someone hidden behind the machine stands punctured the air.

"In billiards, that would be an excellent shot," the Frenchman bragged.

Bolan ignored the comment and stared at where the screams had come from. Fabray started to lift his MAT to his shoulder, but the Executioner reached back and stopped him, holding a finger to his lips.

Five minutes passed. Dead silence.

Then a pair of shadows crawled along a rear wall, heading toward a side door. Bolan could make out the SMGs in their hands.

He waited until they were in the open area between the machines and exterior wall, then shouted, "Now!"

Almost as one, the soldier and French agent got to their feet and fired bursts at the new shadows near the outside wall.

"That should take care of them," the French Intelligence official stated, relaxing his tense grip on the subgun stock.

"Not yet," Bolan replied as he pulled the pin on a grenade and tossed it at four men who raced out of the rear of the factory, wildly firing their AK-47s on full-auto.

Bits of flesh and blood sprayed across the side of the truck as two of the attackers disintegrated.

Two more hardmen rushed into the open area, spraying showers of killer lead from the TEC-9s they held.

"I've got the one on the right," Bolan shouted and, without waiting for Fabray's acknowledgment, carefully placed three shots, then watched as the Corsican gunner sprayed the ceiling with lead from his SMG before crumpling to the floor.

Fabray trained his 9 mm subgun on the other emerging street soldier. Crouched behind a piece of heavy equipment, Fabray could see well enough to empty his magazine into the attacker's midsection, almost cutting him in two.

As quickly as it had begun, the shooting duel stopped.

The Frenchman looked around at the carnage. "That should end their game," he said aloud in satisfaction.

One of the shadows tried to stand, the dim light from outside the factory framing the man.

Bolan started to aim the Uzi, then saw the extent of the gunner's wounds.

The hood tried to raise his weapon, but it slipped from his hands and fell to the floor. Its owner fell on top of it and became a corpse.

A second shadow lay stretched out on the floor. Cautiously Bolan approached the still form. Aiming his Uzi at the squirming body, he saw the fear etched upon the dying gunman's face.

"Kill me," he begged. "I can't endure the pain."

"Where did your boss go?"

"I don't know."

"I can end the pain," the Executioner promised. He had done so many times, even for his enemies.

"Please," the fallen mercenary pleaded.

"Where?"

"Courchevel 1800. At the Everest," the hit man gasped.

Bolan looked at the French agent.

"I know the place. It's very inaccessible. A perfect place for gangsters to hold a meeting. We should leave as soon as possible."

"In a minute," Bolan replied.

The Executioner raised the Uzi, placed it close to the dying man's ear, then fired two rounds.

There was a momentary shudder as the lead tore into the soft tissue of the man's brain, then stillness as the hired thug's body relaxed its grip on life.

Bolan stared at the bodies. Wasted lives.

He felt no sympathy for any of the dead. They received what they had intended to deliver—death.

16

Courchevel, France

The Eurocopter settled down on a small, makeshift heliport in the resort village of Courchevel 1650, located two hundred meters below the resort where Marius and his partners were meeting with the managers of their arms-manufacturing company.

The alpine meadows were covered with a variety of wildflowers. The midday air had a slight nip to it, but the sun encountered no pollution as it spread its brightness across the French Alps.

The only signs of snow were located at the top of the higher peaks.

Fabray had walked across the square and found the local constable, who led the way into a small barred building.

"I must call Paris," Fabray explained to Bolan, then followed the constable into the building.

Ten minutes later he returned to the helicopter, where Bolan was waiting.

"Bad news, *mon ami*. According to the local police, there are more than thirty men meeting at the Hotel Everest. So we have been ordered to wait for a team of attack specialists from my agency to join us."

"How long?"

The Frenchman shrugged.

"As little as eight hours, as much as two days. The wheels of government in France turn slowly."

The Executioner retrieved his canvas bag from the helicopter. "In the meantime I can do some scouting," he said.

"You are not in the employ of the French government, so I cannot stop you. But I must warn you that my government will not take kindly to a foreigner using French soil for his own private war."

Bolan understand. The speech Henri Fabray had just delivered had been memorized from some book of rules and regulations. The soldier had heard the same kind of words said to him in many countries.

"Now, if I can find some transportation," he suggested.

"No problem." The stout Frenchman handed the Executioner a set of keys and pointed to an ancient jeep, modified to operate in the deep snows that winter brought to the Alps. "It's old, but the constable assures me it is sound and fast."

The soldier started to walk across the square to where the surplus military vehicle was parked.

"One more thing. The Hotel Everest is owned by the Union Corse through one of its so-called legal companies."

Bolan nodded as he got behind the wheel.

"I'll get on the telephone and see if I can speed things up," the Frenchman promised.

With as many as thirty professional hardmen to face, the Executioner knew he could use the backup.

MARIUS EXPLODED as the voice on the telephone told him about the destruction of his castle.

"Who did it? I want the man found and killed. Do you understand me?" The Union Corse chief slammed down the telephone and turned to Margaritta Schindler.

Glaring at her, Marius snarled, "What do you know about this?"

The woman looked puzzled. "About what?"

"That was the commander of the Ajaccio police barracks. Someone murdered my men and blew up the castle. Everything is gone. Antiques, furniture, the files and records, clothing, the armory. Everything!"

The former member of the Baader-Meinhof Gang knew this wasn't the right time to complain about the destruction of her extensive Parisian wardrobe, or the jewelry Marius had given her over the three years she had lived with him.

Instead, she focused on the problem. "Does anyone know who did it?"

"Some farmers who saw a big man dressed in black racing a car down the road from the castle as the explosions started," the Union Corse boss growled.

"But who sent him?"

"I'll ask him when we find him," Marius snapped. "And sooner or later we will find him."

"Someone on Corsica had to provide him with information about the castle," Schindler commented, rubbing her chin as she weighed the problem. "Who knew about the castle?"

"People on the island, I suppose," Marius stated. "The police and soldiers on my payroll, of course. To others, the castle is just another ancient building on the road to Mount Cinto."

"Exactly." Schindler thought about the situation, then stared into Marius's face. "Unless somebody told them who really occupied the castle."

"Who would be stupid enough to do that?"

The woman looked around the large lounge area where plant managers were chatting with members of the syndicate's board, under the watchful eyes of two dozen Union Corse armed street soldiers.

Most of the guests were drinking, but none as heavily as Saloman Moussad, the Lebanese representative of Middle

Eastern terrorist groups, and Philip Cambridge, the South African businessman.

Moussad looked to where Marius and Schindler were sitting. He smiled at the blonde, then looked surprised when she gestured for him to join them.

"You look particularly beautiful tonight," he said, trying to hide his interest in her from the Union Corse chief.

"Thank you," she commented, then looked at the glass in Moussad's hand. "Is it wise for a Muslim to drink in public?"

"When the mullahs and their spies are not present, it is a pleasant way to kill an evening," he replied casually, commenting on the Muslim religious leaders.

"I hear you like to gamble a bit at the casinos in Beirut," the woman said softly.

"An innocent diversion."

"Not when you speak so openly about your business after a few drinks."

Moussad became defensive. "That is not true."

"Perhaps not, but that is what I've been told."

Looking offended, the Lebanese businessman turned and strode away.

Philip Cambridge had been watching from across the room. Looking amused, he strolled over to where Schindler and Marius were sitting.

"I see my old friend Moussad got slapped on the wrists," he commented.

The Union Corse boss looked puzzled. "I don't understand what you are trying to say, Mr. Cambridge."

"I was just observing that someone with an ego as big as Saloman's needs to be set straight on a regular basis." He glanced at the crowd. "He's not a team player, you know."

"And you," Marius asked, "are you a team player?"

"Most definitely. Especially where my money's invested."

"Do you ever discuss our business with someone not in our circle?"

Cambridge looked surprised. "Never."

"I just wonder what you and that elderly yacht broker on Corsica..." He turned to the blonde for help.

"William Proger, an American," she added.

Marius nodded gratefully. "What you and Proger talked about when you got together."

Trying to hide his discomfort at the confrontation, the South African replied, "We have dinner and a few drinks, and just talk about this and that. Nothing terribly important."

He looked down at his empty hand. "Which reminds me. I could use a fresh drink."

He walked to the small bar quickly.

Schindler watched him vanish into a crowd of the syndicate's manufacturing managers. Turning to Marius, she observed, "I think you've found two sources of leaks. There may be others."

Marius nodded, then leaned over and whispered, "Perhaps I can count on you to plug up these two leaks while I deal with the others and discuss why we are here."

"What about the American yacht broker? We do not know what Cambridge has told him," she reminded him.

The Union Corse chieftain nodded. "I'd almost forgotten about him. I'll send a pair of men down from Marseilles to shut down that pipeline forever."

Schindler smiled. She hadn't convinced Marius to let her handle the assassination, but at least she would get to kill two capitalists. And like most capitalists, the two men had made their money illegally.

A feeling of being alive ran through her as she stood and walked toward her room, and the pistol she had hidden there.

17

The road to Courchevel was typically alpine, almost too narrow for its two lanes, and steep. In the distance Bolan could see the mountainous resort community and above it the outline of the Everest Hotel.

A large German car was stopped on the side of the road. Bolan slowed his vehicle and glanced inside. The car was empty.

Even from a distance he could see the bloodstains on both front seats. Except for a lack of bodies, it reminded him of the dead couple he had found on the road to Marius's fortress on Corsica.

He stopped the borrowed jeep and pulled to the side of the road.

Getting out, he walked to where the Mercedes-Benz 450 was parked and studied the interior. A book about the wild-flowers of the Alps sat on the front passenger seat. Looking past the car, he saw two freshly formed mounds of earth. There was no need to dig into them. The soldier knew he'd find bodies.

He didn't have to guess who had murdered them. With the gathering of Marius's "board of directors" at the hotel, Bolan knew that this had to be handiwork of the leader of the Union Corse—or his people's.

He had planned to wait for Henri Fabray and the team of DSGE agents, but these murders could be the first of many. He had to move on Marius.

At most he'd wait until dark to make his move.

Returning to his vehicle, the soldier rummaged through his canvas bag and found a pair of Zeiss 10×30 binoculars. Even with their power, Bolan couldn't see any guards patrolling the area.

But he knew they were there. Someone like the head of the Union Corse would never travel without an entourage of armed killers.

Bolan was glad he wore his blacksuit under the rugged tan pants and jacket. In one of his pockets he had a small can of camouflage cosmetics.

The combination would make him less visible at night, when he planned to begin his campaign against Marius and his partners.

The afternoon sun was glaring down on him. But despite the cloudless sky, there was a nip in the air that the Executioner knew never warmed up at this altitude.

While he waited, he retrieved the weapons he planned to carry that night. The silenced 9 mm Beretta 93-R automatic, with its stock folded, was already in its leather shoulder holster under his jacket.

He stripped the .44 Magnum Desert Eagle, carefully cleaning each part, then reassembled the mammoth Israeli semiautomatic pistol and snapped in a full magazine.

A pair of 9 mm mini-Uzis got the same careful treatment, then were carefully placed on the floor of the front of the vehicle, ready to be snapped up and used at a moment's notice.

In many ways the Israeli-made SMG was his most trusted close-quarters combat weapon. It was reliable, rarely jammed and could be fired one-handed, whenever that was necessary.

Strapping a canvas web belt around his waist, Bolan clipped a pair of 40 mm fragmentation grenades to it. Digging through the carryall, he found 40 mm incendiaries and added a pair to the belt.

The Applegate-Fairbairn knife, in its slender sheath, was strapped to his left forearm.

Loading his pockets with extra clips, the Executioner started to zip the bag shut, then made a last-minute decision.

He filled a canvas shoulder bag lying in the carryall with three bricks of plastic explosives after attaching tiny timers and detonators to each one.

Checking the hotel through the powerful lenses, Bolan could see the vague forms of two men walking out of the hotel and onto the veranda. There was no way he could determine who they were, but he could see one of them shove something into the chest of the other man and watch as the man crumpled to the ground.

Bolan knew that he had just witnessed an execution. There was nothing he could do about it. And from what he had heard about the Union Corse chieftain, both of the men he had seen though the binoculars worked for Marius.

He corrected himself. Only one still did. The other was obviously dead.

Climbing back into the driver's seat, Bolan leaned his head back and rested his eyes.

He was ready for this night action and hoped that Marius and his men weren't ready for him.

THE UNION CORSE CHIEF sat at the head table, surrounded by the remaining directors of the syndicate. He waited as the plant managers, and the Corsicans he had assigned to guard them, started to enter the conference room.

Still furious at the destruction of his Corsican castle, he turned to the American Mafia representative to ask a question. "We had some trouble back in Corsica."

Gamboni stared back. "What kind of trouble?"

"Somebody tried to invade my castle and killed a number of my men before getting away," Marius replied.

"That's nothing like the kind of trouble we used to get back in the States from a kill-crazy nut named Mack Bolan. The guy—"

He stopped in the middle of a sentence when he saw the platinum blonde who worked for the Corsican enter the room.

Dressed in a simple outfit that was copied by her Parisian seamstress from a Swiss peasant costume, Margaritta Schindler stepped through the sun-drenched glass doors. The smile on her face had an innocent quality that mocked the hardness she felt inside. With the sun behind her, she looked almost virginal.

Marius saw the hungry expression on the American's face, then turned his head and looked past the seated men at her.

Still smiling, she moved forward and took her seat at the end of the head table, next to the Corsican.

Leaning over, Marius whispered, "Both have been dealt with?"

"Yes. The groups they represent will be notified both died in an automobile accident," she whispered back. "Unfortunately blood from one of them spotted my dress, so I had to change clothes."

"You look wonderful. At least the American thinks so." He nodded at Gamboni.

"And you?"

"More beautiful than ever." The Union Corse head changed the subject. "I wonder who the investors of the two organizations will send to replace them?"

"Men who don't like to boast as much as them, I trust," she replied, then added, "How did the others at the head table take the news?"

"They don't know yet. I've notified them that Cambridge and Moussad received messages to return home immediately and left their proxy votes with me.''

He turned from the woman and looked at the others at the head table and raised his voice.

''Are we ready to begin, gentlemen?''

One by one, the men nodded. The Hong Kong Triad representative leaned his seat back against the wall and studied the men seated in the large conference room. Razid Mansour leaned forward and studied the faces of the plant managers. Salvatore Gamboni glared at the men who ran the various factories, his face reflecting his feeling that all of them were lazy and worthless.

Only Hans Zelnick smiled at them. The expression was automatic with him.

The Union Corse chief turned from his fellow directors and looked at the assembled men.

''You have each received orders to bring your plants up to full capacity. Is that not correct?''

Grumbling, the plant managers nodded.

One of them raised a hand.

Marius pointed to him. ''Is there something you want to ask?''

''Yes,'' the executive replied in a Brazilian accent. ''The orders do not make sense. We don't have orders for half of our current inventory.''

Marius ran his finger down a typewritten list, then looked up again. ''You are Mr. Bahian?''

''Yes. Jose Bahian.''

''Mr. Bahian, we need men who can take orders, not question them.''

He looked at the Corsican seated next to Bahian. ''Is that not right, Mr. Montagne?''

The big man with scars marring his features agreed. ''That is the first rule,'' he replied.

"Then take Mr. Bahian outside and explain it to him again."

Grabbing the Brazilian's arm, Montagne dragged him through the glass doors and onto the patio.

Marius waited until he heard three muffled shots, then looked at the men still in the room. "Is there anyone else who has questions?"

Marius looked around the room. No one dared raise his hand. "Then let us continue."

Before he could say anything else, the burly Corsican hood who had left the conference room with the Brazilian returned.

Alone.

The Union Corse leader raised his head and stared at the man he had called Montagne. "What about Mr. Bahian?"

"Unfortunately he decided to resign his job."

"Then, for now, you will take his place."

The Corsican grunted and sat.

Marius looked at his fellow directors again. All seemed satisfied with his decision.

"As all of you know, your operations have suffered from a lack of demand. The reasons for this are obvious—the actions of the United States government.

"We anticipate a sudden growth in the purchase of the items we manufacture. We expect a flood of orders in pistols, revolvers, rifles, submachine guns and the ammunition for them. We also expect demand for tanks, armed vehicles, missile launchers and missiles, grenades and grenade launchers."

Shaking with fear as he got to his feet, a slightly stooped man speaking with a Bulgarian accent raised his voice. "How can you be so sure we will get many new orders? I would not like to find our warehouse filled with weapons we cannot sell."

Before Marius could answer, another man—this one

speaking English with a thick Irish brogue—spoke. "I don't know if any of the others have run into this problem, but we are being threatened with lawsuits from those companies whose handguns and rifles we've copied."

The Union Corse chief slammed his hand on the table, surprising his fellow directors and the others in the conference room.

"Enough questions," he shouted. "We will take care of selling everything you can make. And we'll deal with those companies who are trying to stop you from making guns."

A short bearded German raised his hand.

Exasperated, Marius snapped, "Yes?"

"You are including my plant in your orders, I assume."

The others stared at the German. It was no secret that in his former East German factory he had manufactured chemical-warfare components, including large quantities of poisons used by the secret police and intelligence services to murder dissidents and enemy officials.

"I predict that very soon the world will return to the time when enemies were killed with weapons—and other things—not hugged at international conferences. But, yes, your plant is very much included in our plans, Herr Stanzig."

"Good," the small man replied. "I will need a few weeks to assemble the chemicals I require. They aren't easily available."

"Not too long," the Union Corse boss warned.

A tall, thin, turbaned Indian was hesitant in raising his hand. Finally he got the courage to speak. "To increase production we will need to acquire more materials. Won't this be considered odd given that the world seems to be disarming?"

Salvatore Gamboni started to laugh. An icy stare from Marius stopped his thin, reedy giggles. The Union Corse head turned back to the Indian questioner. "I can assure you that in a few weeks, disarming will be something no nation will talk about for a very long time.''

Schindler leaned over and whispered in Marius's ear. ''Only if Lushenska lives up to his reputation.''

''I've invited him to fly here for a short conversation tonight,'' the Corsican whispered back. ''And if he fails, there is always you, my dear girl.''

18

The cloudless sky allowed the reflected light from the moon to wash the landscape with a ghostly brightness.

Bolan studied the sky above him for any sign of French government helicopters.

There was none.

The silence that surrounded him was almost deafening.

Bolan moved the jeep closer to the Hotel Everest. Now he could make out the shapes of six men who marched the perimeter of the resort, searching for possible enemies.

The blacksuit and combat cosmetics he wore wouldn't be as effective as they had been on prior missions, where total darkness had made him almost invisible until it was too late.

Moving in the shadows of the alpine evergreens that studded the land around the hotel, the soldier worked his way to the far end of the veranda.

From inside he could hear the sounds of voices. Outside there was only silence until one of the Corsican guards called out loudly, "Luc, is everything quiet?"

"Not even a deer is out here," a voice shouted back.

Looking up at the elevated patio, Bolan saw the husky form of a street soldier. The man was Mafia, albeit Corsican Mafia, and there was no mistaking the bulge of holstered hardware beneath the right arm. Or the 9 mm Ingram Model 10 submachine gun cradled in his arms and fitted with a MAC sound suppressor.

The sound suppressor made no sense to Bolan, given that the rest of the people in the hotel worked for Marius, perhaps including the Everest staff.

The gunman was in his early twenties, but his eyes were those of a hardened killer way beyond his years.

Bolan had to get closer to the slightly opened French doors. His instincts, and the presence of the guards, told him that Marius, his partners and his top lieutenants were inside.

The hardman stood in his way, and the only solution was to render him unconscious—or kill him.

Using the metal railing, Bolan pulled himself up and jumped onto the veranda when the guard had his back turned.

Bolan extended the silenced Beretta 93-R to arm's length, the squat muzzle of its customized sound suppressor almost touching the back of the hardman's neck.

"Drop the gun," the Executioner whispered.

The surprised thug spun and snarled his defiance. "You drop yours," he snapped, staring at the Beretta in Bolan's hand.

As the gunner tried to bring his weapon into play, Bolan stroked the trigger of the 93-R, firing a single round that cored a hole into his adversary's brain. The body slumped against the side of the building, then slid to the floor, brushing a path of blood on its journey downward.

Cat-footing to the French doors, Bolan listened for a moment, then gently opened them slightly. A wide man with a badly botched crew cut tumbled against the soldier, losing his balance and falling to the floor. A second shadowy figure was behind him, and he rushed at Bolan.

Two more men shoved a rear door open and raced forward, waving silenced Heckler & Koch MP-5 K SMGs. The first invader started to get to his feet.

Grasping his attacker's wrist, Bolan used the man's own momentum to send him crashing into the man behind him.

Bolan spun in one fluid movement to fend off the frontal assault by the other two, his right foot continuing on a high arc. The kick connected with the leading thug's rib cage, snapping bone as the would-be killer was driven back against the door frame.

The second hood tried to jump on the Executioner's back and pull him to the floor. But Bolan focused his energy in the edge of his right palm as he twisted and slashed it against his assailant's carotid artery. With only a small whoosh to signal his death, the hardman fell backward against his partner.

Pushing his dead comrade from him, the gangster reached for a long-bladed knife he'd hidden in his waistband, then rushed at his adversary, cursing as he held the blade in the air, ready to slash at the American.

Bolan let him get closer, then stepped aside and twisted the man's knife hand. Struggling, the tough tried to twist his hand free from the Executioner's grip. As he strained, concentrating every ounce of his nearly three hundred pounds in his effort to pull away, the hood broke out in a sweat. Veins on both sides of his head popped out and threatened to burst.

Bolan let the tough's strength do the majority of the work, just making sure the blade didn't get any closer.

Finally the thug gasped for air, then began to resume the battle. To his horror the hand that held the razor-sharp blade refused to do his bidding. Inch by inch it started pushing back to his face, guided there by his adversary's hand.

He knew he had to break away, but the American wouldn't let him go. He felt the blade touch his jacket, then pierce through it and his shirt.

With one last, desperate effort, he used both hands to

push the man away, then felt the blade slice beneath his skin and through his ribs.

As the blade moved upward toward his aorta, the Union Corse hardman thought of all the mistakes he had made in his life. Then, as light and consciousness began to fade, he knew this was the last one he'd ever make.

Bolan let the man slide to the floor, his blood forming a pool in which he lay.

A man appeared at the front door, clutching a 9 mm parabellum Bernadelli P-O18 pistol in his left hand. "Luc, Leon, Flick," he called out. "Where the hell are you?"

He stopped talking when he saw the bodies of his companions on the floor. Then he looked up and stared at the cold face of the man who stood in front of him.

He snapped his pistol into firing position, but it was too little too late. The pointed tip of the blade Bolan had thrown tore into his throat, and he fell, in agony, onto the veranda. A mercy round from the Beretta ended his suffering.

For the moment, the Executioner was surrounded only by the dead. But he knew someone would be coming out to check on them shortly.

AT LUSHENSKA'S REQUEST, Marius had agreed to meet the Russian in a small, isolated cottage a short distance from the main hotel structure. Except for the two men, only Margaritta Schindler would be present.

"The fewer who see my face, the better it is for both my clients and me," the Russian had said when he agreed to meet and discuss the assignment.

A modified version of the SA 342M Gazelle helicopter was parked outside the small house.

The pilot, formerly a Russian air force officer, was on Lushenska's payroll.

The Union Corse chief had started to explain the reason for the assassination. The Russian stopped him with a raised hand. "We do not bother with why. Only with what, and how much it will cost."

With a smile the Corsican changed the subject and raised his glass of wine. "Then good hunting," he said. "I presume you've selected the person to carry out our assignment."

Lushenska smiled. He had gotten a call from Rudy Johnson from Paris before he had left for the Alps. The former CIA official had said it was urgent that they meet as soon as possible.

His contacts had told him about Johnson's termination and his personal need for revenge. Who would be more perfect for the job than someone the President knew personally?

"I am meeting with him late tonight," Lushenska replied.

The Russian knew that Johnson was flying into Geneva even as he was meeting with the client and his mistress.

He could imagine what Johnson wanted—to take Hawthorne's place as a partner.

The Union Corse chieftain interrupted the Russian's thoughts. "Any ideas on how and where the killing will be handled?"

"Where is obvious. In Brussels, before or after the American President meets with the other NATO officials."

He paused. "How is a little more difficult. Shooting him would be relatively difficult. He will be surrounded by his own guards, as well as a great number of other security men and women. We are seriously considering the use of ricin."

Marius looked surprised. "One of our plants still makes the poison, but I thought that with the end of the Cold War, nobody used it."

Lushenska nodded. Covert agents had stabbed dissidents living in foreign countries with sharp objects coated with the toxin, using such common objects as umbrellas, canes and hairpins to inject the deadly liquid.

"If somebody the President knew well were to reach out to shake his hand, it would be possible to conceal a metal needle coated with ricin and scratch the American leader with it."

"Will that look like an assassination attempt?"

"Not necessarily. But we will have someone kill him with a bullet from a sniper's rifle at the same time. That should be evidence enough."

The Union Corse boss glanced at Schindler, then turned back to the Russian. "I would like that backup to be Margaritta."

Schindler looked stunned. And pleased.

Lushenska was speechless for a moment, then remembered what he knew of the woman's history. He made an instant decision. Why not? From what he knew of her, she was equal to, if not better than, the best of the agents he had used for such assignments.

"The balance of our fee—" he started to say.

"Herr Zelnick will leave with the two of you. In fact he is probably already on board. He is authorized to release the money for the rest of your fee when you are finished."

THE CORSICAN WAS WRONG. The Swiss banker had stopped in the lobby and asked where he could find the nearest telephone.

One of the guards pointed to the manager's office.

Taking a chance, Zelnick decided that the arms syndicate desperately needed a change of leadership. He lifted the phone and dialed the operator.

"What is the telephone number of the police?"

She offered to connect him.

The Swiss banker took a deep breath and tried to hide his accent.

"I was driving by the Hotel Everest this evening," he reported. "I tried to rent a room, but I saw a great number of foreign-looking men, all carrying guns. They looked like criminals."

He listened to a question and replied, "At least twenty. Probably more. I don't know what they are doing here, but I can't believe it's anything honest."

"Thank you for the information," the officer on the end replied. "I will notify my chief. I'm sure he will want to investigate."

Zelnick hung up the phone and hurried to where the helicopter was waiting.

MARIUS CHECKED the gold-and-diamond-studded Rolex watch on his wrist.

"I would suggest that the two of you join Herr Zelnick."

He turned to Schindler. "I had a maid pack your bags. They are aboard the helicopter. You will need to get the best weapons to carry in case they are needed. But I am sure Mr. Lushenska can get you anything you need in Geneva." He stared meaningfully at the Russian.

As he held out his hand to help the blonde to her feet, Viktor Lushenska understood the unspoken message from the Corsican.

Succeed or die.

THE SUDDEN WHIRRING of helicopter blades distracted the Executioner. As he watched the small chopper climb above the building, he regretted that he hadn't thought to bring one of the Russian-made RPG-7 launchers and several PG-7M HEAT rockets he had found in the Corsican fortress's armory.

Bolan's main concern was that the Union Corse chief was escaping. But that concern evaporated with the sound of somebody pushing open one of the French doors.

GERMAIN HAD COME outside to make sure that the guards weren't loafing. Marius had assigned him the job of security chief.

As he started to the doors behind him, he became aware of the silence outside. It was unusual for Corsicans to be quiet. They had a need to keep talking, to make fun of one another and to brag about their latest exploits.

He looked around and spotted the bodies scattered about the veranda.

As he raised his eyes from the floor, he became aware of a dark presence.

One of the shadows on the brick wall began to move away from the others. It was a man, carrying an Uzi SMG gripped in his left hand.

Germain had no choice. He turned and raced around the corner of the main building, using the darkness to protect himself.

BOLAN STARTED to give chase, but halted when he heard a French-accented voice call out.

"We are here, my friend."

Bolan turned. Henri Fabray was standing there, a MAT subgun in his hands. Behind him were eight armed men in combat fatigues and a large number of uniformed policemen.

The reinforcements had arrived.

19

Mack Bolan quickly summarized the situation for the Frenchman, then concluded, "I see you decided to invite the local police to help."

Fabray shook his head. "That is what is so odd. We stopped ten of them on the road and asked where they were going. Their chief said they had gotten a call and were heading here to investigate. So we invited them to join us."

Bolan wondered who had called them. An innocent bystander? He didn't think so. More likely one of Marius's directors, deciding to get even for some real or fancied injustice.

This wasn't the time to give the identity of the caller any thought. He had a battle to fight.

"One of Marius's men just took off. I'm going after him," Bolan stated.

"And me with you," the Frenchman replied. He turned to one of his team and issued a stream of orders in French.

As BOLAN and the Frenchman rounded the corner, they could see the hardman rush through a door, and heard a woman scream.

The Executioner moved cautiously to a window near the door and peered over the sill. His prey had run into the hotel's kitchen. Bolan could see he had pushed the snout of his Browning semiautomatic pistol against the face of a terrified gray-haired woman wearing a chef's apron.

The woman spoke hysterically in French. "Please don't kill me. I have a husband and children and grandchildren. Please don't hurt me."

Bolan was thinking of how he could separate the gunman from the woman when he sensed someone behind him. He turned and looked, his Uzi gripped firmly in his hand.

It was Fabray.

Bolan lowered the gun and pointed to the window. "Looks like a standoff. If he gets it, so does she."

"I have a suggestion," the DSGE official whispered back. Quickly he outlined it.

"It could work," Bolan agreed.

The Frenchman slipped away to carry out his part.

Bolan rose to his feet, making sure he couldn't be seen from inside. Luckily the window had been left open to circulate fresh air into the kitchen.

He looked around and spotted an empty wooden box. Quickly he carried it to the window.

He could hear the heavy banging on the front door. The gunman tightened his grip on the elderly woman.

"Who is it?"

The voice outside shouted in French, "I have a delivery of vegetables."

"Tell him to come back tomorrow," Germain whispered.

The woman did as he ordered.

Fabray called out again. "I can't. As you know, we come up here only once a week."

The gunman forced the woman to walk in front of him as they moved slowly toward the front door. Bolan mounted the box and silently slipped in through the window. Cat-footing, he moved behind the gunman, the Uzi subgun in his hand ready to spit death.

"Open the door," the gunman ordered.

As the woman began to turn the doorknob, Bolan crept

up behind the gunman and pushed the SMG close to his ear. This was a killer, he reminded himself as he pulled the trigger with one hand and knocked down the pistol with the other.

A short burst of 9 mm rounds punctured the tiled floor as Fabray shoved the door open and rushed in, pointing his pistol at the body on the ground.

Bolan's bullet had torn up the brain tissue. Blood and tissue began to ooze through the hole created by the 9 mm round.

The woman turned, stared at the dead gunman and collapsed.

The Frenchman caught her before she hit the floor.

"Mother Mary," she gasped in French.

"She was looking after you," Fabray whispered as he lowered her to the tiles.

THE SOUNDS OF GUNFIRE being exchanged punctured the night.

Bolan raced toward the noises, followed closely by Fabray. The man was surprisingly fast, despite the prosthesis he wore to replace his missing leg.

Two of the DSGE agents were dead, but the other six were pouring round after round of deadly lead into the conference room inside the hotel.

The screams of wounded and dying men rang in the Executioner's ear as he knelt next to the DSGE agent Fabray had placed in charge.

"The Union Corse boss. Have you seen him?"

Without turning his head from the assault weapon braced against his shoulder, the young attack specialist shook his head. "Not yet. Only these thugs," he muttered as he focused his weapon on a tall, snarling street soldier who was trying to snap a fresh clip into his Ingram MAC-10. A pair of 5.56 mm hollowpoint rounds erupted out of the FA MAS carbine and tore a cavity in the Union Corse thug's chest.

Bolan searched the patio with his eyes.

No Marius.

"Perhaps he's hiding someplace inside," Fabray suggested.

MARIUS GLANCED AROUND at the confusion and killings, and decided to leave before whoever was attacking his men caught him, as well. He ran from the hotel to the vehicles in the rear parking lot.

The Union Corse chief looked in the front window of one of the cars, a souped-up 1965 Oldsmobile that was the joy of the hotel's head chef. The keys were in the ignition.

Pulling the door open, Marius jumped into the driver's seat and keyed the ignition. The engine coughed but refused to start. He kept trying, until finally he heard an explosion and the engine was running.

The stench of burned gunpowder had permeated the vehicle. Marius rolled down his window and put the car in reverse. All he could think about was getting away from the wholesale mayhem around him. He'd worry about where to go and what to do after he got on the tarred road. He hadn't survived all these years to die in some wretched remote corner of the French Alps.

A tall husky man stood in his path as he turned the car around and raced for the dirt road that led to the lower resorts and safety. It was one of the French agents. The man held up a hand for him to stop, but Marius trod on the accelerator and tried to hit him.

When the intelligence officer moved to the right and grabbed on to the door handle, Marius gunned the car and dragged the man along. He could hear the Frenchman hammering on the metal door. Then, suddenly, there was no more hammering.

The Union Corse chief looked out of the rearview mirror. The French agent's body lay in the middle of the dirt road. Another man—stout and older—rushed into the roadway and knelt next to the body.

Turning away, Marius looked down at the road and saw a tall dark-haired man standing in his path, holding an Uzi. Nobody was going to stop him. He aimed the car at his assailant, who had braced the subgun against his midsection and was firing round after round.

The windshield finally shattered under the pressure of the lead slugs. Marius swerved the car as he ducked his head out of the path of the flying shards.

The stolen car went out of control as the Union Corse leader tried to regain control. His foot seemed frozen on the accelerator as he twisted the steering wheel.

A stand of trees loomed up directly in front of him. Panicked, he tore open the driver's door and dived out of the vehicle just before it impacted with the trunk of a sturdy evergreen.

Stunned, he pulled himself to his feet. His 9 mm H&K P-7 pistol had fallen to the ground. He stooped and picked it up, only to hear a voice call out to him.

"Drop it."

He looked up. It was the dark-haired stranger, whose Uzi was now focused on him.

Marius thought quickly. He let his hand open as he clicked off the safety on the automatic, then twisted it up and fired at the ominous-looking intruder.

The Executioner fanned a burst of shots at the well-dressed gang chief, almost severing his right hand, before the man could complete his trigger action. Marius was shocked as he looked at his damaged hand and the blood dripping onto the ground from a ruptured artery.

He tried to grab his automatic in his other hand. Bolan

fired a second burst, puncturing the breadth of the man's midsection.

Marius fell forward, collapsing on a pool of his own blood.

A uniformed police lieutenant watched the Union Corse chief fall, then walked back to the hotel to make a call.

Bolan wasted no time in examining the body. There were more Union Corse killers to destroy.

20

Bolan found Fabray.

"I'm checking the upstairs," he said. "Just in case somebody's hiding up there."

The Frenchman looked at the carnage of the battle. "How many more can be left?"

"I'll feel better knowing there isn't anyone," the warrior said.

"I'll follow you upstairs as soon as we finish down here," the stout Frenchman promised.

THE BACK STAIRS of the hotel seemed deserted as Bolan moved toward them. He knew that someplace in the darkness there could be Union Corse thugs, waiting to kill him.

The soldier wasn't fooled by the lack of noise. Attempts to lull him into similar traps had been tried before. The hotel provided a plethora of hiding places for assassins, such as behind any of the doors on the main floor or upstairs.

He moved cautiously across the hotel lobby, trying to maintain silence. But even with the rubber-soled shoes he was wearing, he could hear the quiet suction sounds of his feet as he approached the flight of stairs. The vast open space exaggerated the noise of his movements.

He stopped short when he heard a shuffling noise from above him. Glancing up, he saw the shadow of a figure carrying a TEC-9.

There was no time for Bolan to aim. He swung up his Uzi and squeezed off three rounds, which tore into walls on the floor above him.

From behind him he heard movement of booted feet moving toward him.

The Executioner tore a 40 mm fragmentation grenade from his canvas belt, pulled the pin and threw the multigrooved bomb in a slow loping spin at the trio of Corsicans who had tried to sneak up on him from behind.

Then Bolan threw himself behind a heavy credenza.

The interior of the hotel lobby shattered as the frag grenade exploded, flinging metal fragments of death in every direction.

He could hear the screams of dying men and smell something burning. As he waited behind the credenza, the soldier could see a small fire starting to burn in the nearest couch.

Four men sprinted into the lobby. They paused for a brief moment to glance at the shredded bodies of their dead compatriots, then searched for Bolan.

The soldier eased himself from behind the credenza and set the Uzi on continuous fire.

The hardmen charged at him with no concern for their own welfare, firing on the run. They were easy targets, and precise bursts from the Israeli-made subgun punched them to the floor.

Cautiously Bolan moved back to the stairs and started up on the far left side. He stopped frequently to listen and to survey the area ahead. There was a soft, squishy sound in front of him. The wind? He couldn't take a chance that it wasn't, and fired one warning shot from the Uzi.

The shot got results. He heard a door open and slam shut.

Bolan headed for the door, which belonged to one of the housekeeping storerooms. Standing to one side, he carefully edged the door open, then waited. There was no reaction from inside—no shot, no sounds, nothing. Cautiously he peered around the edge, but saw no one.

He slipped inside and moved quickly to the opposite wall, flattening his back against it as he steadied his gun with both hands. He studied the area. It was a typical storeroom, filled with fresh linen and bathroom supplies.

Edging around the wall, he worked his way to a position where he could see some of the corridor.

No one was visible, but he could hear the soft sounds of men hiding in doorways, waiting for him to show himself.

His Uzi needed a fresh magazine, but there wasn't enough time to search his pockets for one.

As he eased the .44 Magnum Desert Eagle out of its holster, the soldier unclipped one of the incendiary grenades on his belt. Jerking free its pin, he rolled the grenade down the corridor, then dived back into the storeroom and squeezed against the far wall.

There was a sudden flash of light and a wave of extreme heat as the grenade exploded. He could hear the pitiful screams of burning men. For the moment they sounded too busy dying to worry about him.

Bolan hurried from the storeroom and headed for the stairs, taking them slowly, stopping at every other step to listen. He heard the sound of someone trying to twist a doorknob, followed by whispered curses. The soldier stopped and waited.

The only way out was back down the stairs.

Whoever it was ran up another flight of stairs. Bolan could hear the same sounds repeated. Suddenly a muffled explosion of bullets smashing against steel rang out.

The gunner was using a sound suppressor, Bolan decided.

The Executioner waited for the gunman to discover that he was trapped. Obviously he had tried to open a metal door that led to the roof. There was nowhere else to go.

Bolan climbed to the next landing, leaned against the wall and took the time to reload his Israeli SMG.

He listened carefully for sounds of the man coming back down the stairs. There was only a soft, brushing noise, like air flowing from vents.

The stench of burning fabric, wood and human flesh wafted up in small clouds of black smoke. The big American could hear the shouts below him as Marius's men tried to quench the fire.

Bolan waited patiently. Any moment now, the man he'd been following would have to come down the stairs.

Moments felt like hours as he waited and listened.

Where was the gunman?

The brushing noise was suddenly louder. Bolan looked up and saw the legs of the gunman as he slowly moved down the steps. Bolan studied them and knew what the brushing sound was. The man wore rubber-soled shoes.

"Drop your gun and come down with your hands up," Bolan commanded.

The feet moved back against the wall. Bolan could no longer see them from where he was standing. He waited, but there was no movement from the other man. Unless the guy came out firing, Bolan didn't want to kill him. There were questions he needed answered, such as where were the other directors? Who had been hired to kill the President?

He could hear the gunman shuffling his feet, trying to decide on his next move. Bolan moved slightly so he could see farther up the stairs.

Suddenly a man rushed at him, his weapon firing as he ran. Bolan twisted away as the bullets smashed into the wall behind him.

He aimed for the man's chest and squeezed the trigger, the bullet striking the gunman just below his breastbone.

He staggered back, shaken by the impact, then fired at Bolan again.

The Executioner knew he had placed the shot perfectly and realized his adversary had to be wearing body armor. He thought he recognized the well-dressed thug. He looked a lot like Salvatore Gamboni, a former street soldier who was part of the Mafia Family that controlled the West Side of Los Angeles.

Knowing he needed to score a head shot, Bolan tilted his weapon and fired twice point-blank into Gamboni's face. With grim satisfaction he saw blood spurt from the two holes in the gunman's forehead.

The gunman stood frozen in place, unwilling to collapse. His hand still gripped his automatic, its ugly snout pointing at Bolan. His trigger finger suddenly contracted in a last muscular reaction.

Bolan felt the heat of the bullet that burst from the weapon as it tore its way into his flesh. He could feel the warm wetness of his blood running down his arm.

The other man sank slowly to the stairs and fell over. The soldier held his gun ready, in case the gunman was still able to fight.

A ground-floor door opened, and a young French agent approached Bolan on the stairs.

"It is all right, *monsieur*," the agent said gently. "Take it easy. You'll be okay." He helped Bolan sit on the floor and leaned him against the thick concrete wall.

The light was breaking up into thousands of pinpoints of glitter. Bolan realized he was hurting and tired, and knew he had to have lost a lot of blood. His eyelids were becoming too heavy to keep open. He didn't fight the curtain of darkness as it descended over his consciousness.

VIKTOR LUSHENSKA had been waiting in his Mercedes-Benz 500 SL for the American to come through the customs doors of Geneva's international airport. For a moment the Russian wondered if his visitor had changed his mind about coming.

Then he saw a sullen-faced man, carrying a large heavy suitcase, struggle toward the curb.

Several cabdrivers tried to entice him into their vehicles, but Rudy Johnson ignored them and searched for the Russian's car.

Lushenska started the engine and pulled up to where the former CIA man was standing.

"Welcome to Geneva," the Russian called out in his slightly accented English.

Without replying, the American opened a rear door and placed his suitcase on the seat. He then closed the door and climbed into the front passenger seat. Like the cautious man he was, Johnson searched for the seat belt and locked it around him.

The Russian smiled as he watched the American settle back in his seat. "Always the careful man, Mr. Johnson?"

The former CIA official ignored the remark. "I'd like to talk someplace where no one can see or hear us."

"My office is perfect. Everyone has already gone home."

Johnson had a look of concern on his face. "I'd prefer some other location," he commented.

Lushenska weighed the request. The blond woman was meeting with Kammil Agca and a gun dealer to select the weapons she would carry to Brussels. He had promised to take her to dinner.

"Unfortunately I have a need to be in my office this evening."

With an expression of surrender, the American agreed to the meeting place.

"Is there a rear entrance to your office building?"

The Russian understood the man's concern. In the world

in which both of them had lived, everybody was watching everybody else.

"We'll take the elevator from the garage to my floor. If anybody is snooping, I will know it immediately, and you will be able to leave before you can be identified."

With a sigh of relief, the American nodded his agreement.

Lushenska smiled to himself. How typical Johnson was. So worried about being found out, but no concern about having somebody killed.

Sometimes, the Russian remembered, he had envied soldiers who fought and died nobly, free of the need to hide their identity or intentions.

That was, he envied them until he checked the large balance in his Swiss bank account.

21

The former KGB general leaned back in his large leather chair and studied the American.

"On the telephone you said it was vital that the two of us meet in person, as soon as possible," Lushenska reminded his visitor, sounding completely relaxed. "What could be so urgent?"

"I have something you want, and you have something I need," the American said, scanning the room for any visible signs of eavesdropping equipment.

"And what is it you have?"

"Contacts. Over the years, directly or through the men who personally reported to me—like Nate Hawthorne—"

The Russian interrupted. "Excellent man. I still have people trying to find the men who killed him and his wife. And his niece, Sally."

His voice became heavy with sadness. "She was almost a daughter to me. My late wife could not have children, so I adopted Sally Hawthorne as the child we never had."

"As I was saying," Johnson continued, sounding irritated at the interruption, "in what I suspect is your business, I believe you need clients. I think I can convince a number of foreign organizations to make use of your services."

"Everybody needs intelligence, especially now when the intelligence branches of many governments have shrunk to where they are valueless."

Johnson smiled coldly. "I believe you sell more than intelligence, Mr. Lushenska. Given your background, I would think you offer a more practical service to your clients."

The Russian leaned forward and stared into the American's face. Sometimes, like now, he missed the power he'd had with the KGB, when the only times he dealt with Americans like Johnson were from the end of an automatic weapon. He sighed in nostalgia. So many memories of being one of the leaders of the Soviet Union's Committee for State Security, before the weaklings took over the government and destroyed the carefully assembled union of republics.

The only way to deal with someone like Johnson was to be blunt, he decided.

"Neither of us have to speculate on the main service we offer our clients. The elimination of enemies."

"Both of us have been in charge of that function during our time with our governments."

"Interesting, but not very useful." Lushenska took a deep breath before continuing. "We get all the clients we need right now. What else are you offering?"

Johnson appeared puzzled. "I'm offering to take Nate Hawthorne's place as your partner."

Lushenska smiled. "Now I understand, Mr. Johnson. But Nate had to prove himself before he became a fifty percent owner of this firm."

"I don't understand."

"Of course Nate had to have contacts for new business, and he knew a great many currently unemployed professionals who were willing to work for us. But first he had to show he had what it takes, as you Americans are so fond of saying."

"How?"

"Do you recall the death of the Sri Lanka candidate for president?"

Johnson thought about it for a few minutes, then nodded. "I remember. We all supposed a Tamil Tiger had killed him."

"Perhaps they paid for his death, but it was one of our staff who did the actual killing."

"And Nate found the right assassin?"

"No, Nate *was* the assassin."

Johnson looked stunned. "Nate?"

"That's how he got to be my partner."

"I wouldn't have suspected that he had the—"

Lushenska interrupted. "The question is, Mr. Johnson, do you have it?"

There was a long pause. Finally the American answered. "I suppose it would depend on whom I had to assassinate."

"The President of the United States?"

Johnson jumped to his feet. "That's an impossible assignment."

The Russian watched as Johnson marched around the room.

"Because of your personal acquaintance with the President?"

"No, not just that," the American replied. "Because he's always well guarded."

"From his friends, too?"

The former CIA official stared at the Russian, then returned and sat on the edge of his chair.

"How can this be done without the assassin getting killed or becoming a hunted man for the rest of his life?"

Lushenska opened a drawer in his desk and withdrew a tiny box.

"It's quite simple," he said as he took off the cover and held up a tiny vial.

"In this vial is a quantity of ricin." He smiled at Johnson. "You do know about ricin?"

The American nodded. "A deadly poison used by the KGB for many years to kill when a gun or a knife would be difficult to use."

"This is a much improved version. A tiny amount injected under the skin works within minutes. And after fifteen minutes it is impossible to detect."

The Russian took out an ornate ring from the small box. "And what is this?"

The former CIA man was confused. "A ring."

"Not just a ring," Lushenska said. "Give me your hand."

Nervously Johnson held out his hand. The Russian ran the ring along the skin on the back of the American's right hand.

"Ouch," Johnson said. "There's a rough edge to the ring."

"Exactly."

The American stared at his hand in horror.

"You mean you've injected ricin into my system?"

"No, no," the Russian assured him. "The ring is perfectly sterile." He paused before adding, "For now."

"How is someone supposed to inject the poison into the President's system?"

"Like I did. If an old acquaintance happened to be in Brussels when the President arrived and reached to shake your leader's hand, I would think that, with so many cameras recording the encounter, he would have no choice but to shake his hand. A slight squeeze of the hand should force the minuscule needle in the ring to penetrate the skin and introduce the ricin."

"It sounds so...cold-blooded."

"That is what we do for a living, Mr. Johnson. Kill people." He saw the expression of disgust on the American's face. "We are not children. Both of us have ordered all kinds of people killed. Even children, if their death would help our countries," he reminded him.

"Somebody would figure out that I was the cause of his death," Johnson said, sounding worried.

"First of all, you will be long gone from Brussels when it is finally discovered he died of poisoning. Second, what is it you Americans say about your politicians?" He thought for a moment and remembered the expression. "Oh, yes. They are always pressing the flesh of everyone around them."

"I'll have to give this some thought."

"Not too long, Mr. Johnson. We need to be in Brussels late tonight. The President arrives tomorrow."

A knock on the door of Lushenska's private office stopped the conversation. He raised his head and stared at the ornate entrance. "Come in."

The door opened, and Margaritta Schindler entered the room, lugging a large leather bag in her left hand.

"I didn't know you were busy. I'll wait outside," she offered.

"No. Come in and join us, Margaritta."

The woman eased into an empty chair near the desk.

Lushenska pointed to Johnson and started to make introductions.

"This is...Mr. Jones. The lady is Miss Smith."

Johnson kept staring at the vial and ring. Finally he lifted his head and looked at the Russian. "I presume there is a substantial amount being paid for the assignment," Johnson said, ignoring the woman.

"You wouldn't earn the amount you will receive if you spent the rest of your life working for your government."

The American took his time before he answered. Finally he took a deep breath. "Consider me your new partner," he said hoarsely.

"After you complete the assignment."

"Agreed," Johnson replied.

"The lady sitting with us will be your backup. If for some reason it is impossible for you to shake the hand of the President, she will make sure we fulfill our agreement."

He turned to Schindler. "Are you ready?"

She reached into the bag and pulled out a compact 9 mm Walther PPK pistol, fitted with a sound suppressor.

"It fits nicely into my purse," she said in reply. "I also acquired an excellent sniper's rifle with a scope."

Johnson interrupted. "Is there a rest room nearby?"

Lushenska reached into his pocket and took out a key. "It's just down the hall, to the right," he said, handing the key over.

As the former intelligence officer left, the Russian picked up the telephone on his desk and dialed a number.

"Kammil? I need for you and perhaps three of your associates to keep watch over the offices while I am away on business." He paused. "Can you be here in a half hour?"

There was another pause as the Turk on the other end replied.

"Good. I should be back from Brussels late tomorrow."

Lushenska paused and looked surprised. "Really? How do you know?"

He listened, then said, "That's interesting. Make sure we deposit a reward to his account."

As he replaced the receiver, he turned to Schindler. "A police lieutenant in Courchevel who trades information called one of my men with the news. Alexander Marius is dead. So are almost all of his men."

The blond woman looked stunned. "When? Where?"

"Somebody called the police to inform them his group was meeting at the Everest Hotel. They showed up after we and Zelnick left." He opened his center drawer, took out a blurry picture and handed it to her.

"By this man. He was photographed by one of our people in Beruba. He took out our assassins. Do you know him?"

She shook her head and was about to say something when the phone rang. Lushenska answered it.

"Yes, Mr. Zelnick. I heard." He stopped and listened for a few minutes. "Who is the new head of your syndicate?" He smiled. "Do you want us to complete the assignment?"

He listened to the reply, then said, "Good. We should have it finished by tomorrow. Please have the money ready."

As an afterthought he added, "I do not believe it would serve your group's purpose if the American President merely had what appeared to be a heart attack. He has to be obviously assassinated."

"I'm glad you agree," Lushenska concluded when consent for his proposal was given. As he hung up the telephone, he smiled at the woman. "It seems there is a new head of the arms syndicate." Schindler looked surprised. "Who?"

"The Swiss banker is taking over."

"Then it would seem I am unemployed. The prospect of having to sleep with that cold fish again is sickening."

"There is room in my organization for someone with your talents," Lushenska said casually.

The woman smiled, then said, "I saw the vial and ring. I presume the vial contained ricin or a similar toxin."

"So far as the American knows, that is how we plan to kill the President of the United States," Lushenska replied.

"What do you have in mind?"

"Let the American be a distraction while you carry out the assassination."

"The American assumes he will become your partner after Brussels."

"If he lives, he will. His future depends on what you decide to do about his ambition."

The woman studied the German-made gun in her hand. "I have some definite ideas about that."

Johnson entered Lushenska's office. He saw the blurry photograph on the Russian's desk and picked it up.

"I know this man," he said angrily. "He's a dangerous psychopath."

"He calls himself Mike Belasko," Lushenska said. "I've made arrangements to have some of the best mercenaries in Brussels meet every plane and train that comes into the city. Anyone who even remotely looks like Belasko will be killed."

He stood and walked toward the ornate door that led out of his office. "I suggest we catch the late flight to Brussels."

22

Hal Brognola sat across the aisle from the President. *Air Force One* was traveling at near supersonic speed, carrying them and the various government specialists on the customized jet to Brussels.

He glanced out of his window. In the dark he could see the lights of Washington, D.C., grow dimmer as the jet started its journey across the Atlantic Ocean.

The Chief Executive leaned across the aisle and asked, "Anything new from your man, Hal?"

Brognola handed the President a copy of the *New York Times* he had picked up at a newsstand before he drove to Andrews Air Force Base.

There was a headline that covered two columns on the lower half of the front page: Wholesale Massacre In French Ski Resort.

The head of the American government skimmed the story, then nodded as he handed the newspaper back to Brognola.

"Sounds like your man made some headway. Any news about the assassin?"

Brognola knew that despite the calmness in the President's voice, he was concerned.

"Last message from him was that he was flying to Geneva. His hunch is that the assassin used it as his base of operations."

"I hope your man can stop him. If not for the country's sake, for the sake of me and my family."

"So do I, Mr. President. So do I," Brognola replied.

He knew that if anyone could find and stop the assassin, Mack Bolan could. When the Executioner had called him from a pay telephone in a small mountain village, they couldn't really talk. The phone wasn't secured.

But he did say that the arms syndicate had been destroyed, and that he believed they had hired the assassin. The problem, according to Bolan, was that none of the men who could identify the killer was still alive.

It was up to the Executioner to find out who the assassin was and to stop him or her before the assassin could reach the President.

A SERIES OF HELICOPTERS came and went in the dark, loaded with the bodies of the dead. Uniformed police officers airlifted those still alive and in handcuffs to Mulhouse, where Bolan knew they would be interrogated.

Marius's empire was in shambles, at least for the moment. Most of the gang representatives who were directors of the arms syndicate had been identified.

All of them were dead, killed by Bolan or in the violent cross-fire between the French attack team and the Corsican gunmen who were guarding the hotel and its occupants.

In all, the soldier counted forty-five bodies. Only two of them were French Intelligence agents.

Fabray sat in an easy chair in the lobby and watched as a military doctor finished treating Bolan's wounds.

"You should spend a few days in a hospital," the doctor suggested.

"Another time," Bolan replied, then thanked the doctor for his help.

When they were alone, he asked the Frenchman if he

had gotten any clues as to the identity of the assassin the dead Union Corse chieftain had hired.

"None of the plant managers knew about the assassination. At least all those still living claimed that Marius never told them about his plans." Fabray sighed as he thought of Marius. "And you killed the one man who could have told us."

"There wasn't time to question him."

"I know," the French official replied. "I wish he would have kept notes about his plans, like most heads of big commercial organizations do."

He studied the soldier's expression of frustration, then said, "There is some good news. The director of my agency has been in touch with his equivalents in the various countries where the syndicate's plants operated. All of them will be seized by morning and put out of business."

The Executioner took the news without reaction. Fabray leaned his head close to Bolan's.

"The doctor is right, you know. You should take some time off to let your wounds heal."

"Later."

The Frenchman sighed. He had known what the answer would be before he asked.

"So what is your next move?"

"I guess I'll have to go to Geneva and hope I can get some information from a Russian named Lushenska."

"The former KGB general?"

Bolan nodded.

"Bad person to confront. As I remember from my days in the field, he always surrounded himself with teams of professional killers."

"Maybe I can catch him on their night off."

"Just don't catch one of their bullets."

Bolan forced a smile onto his face. Death wasn't a requirement in his world. But it was always a reality.

"I can get you through Swiss customs. After that, you are on your own," the Frenchman warned.

Being alone in combat was nothing new for Bolan. It was often preferable to having a horde of well-meaning helpers get themselves killed.

"You may want to replenish your armory," Fabray suggested. "The Corsicans had more weapons with them than most small countries own."

Bolan got to his feet and studied the array of arms out on the veranda. Finally he selected one of the Ingram automatic machine pistols. He knew that they were capable of dumping a 30-round clip in less than ten seconds. He searched through the pile of full magazines the French agents had assembled and found several loaded clips.

He glanced at Fabray. "Teflon coated?"

The Frenchman picked up one of the magazines and studied the bullets. "Better. Glaser rounds. They'll cut through anything that isn't an inch of cold steel," Fabray promised.

Geneva

WEARING THE INGRAM MAC-10 on a leather shoulder strap under his jacket, Bolan checked the offices in the suite. They were empty, except for the one at the end of the corridor. He could hear voices behind it.

"When is the Russian coming back?"

"When he feels the job is done," another voice answered.

"So why are we hanging around here?" someone else asked.

"Because Lushenska is paying us to make sure nobody tries to break in and steal his files."

Bolan checked the Ingram MAC-10, then rammed his

shoulder against the door and shoved it open to confront three men sitting around a folding table.

"Put your guns on the table," he snapped.

He waited for the trio to obey the order. Instead, one of them—a slight man with olive skin—smiled a cold smile of hate. The soldier watched the man's hand as it inched toward the pistol resting on the table.

The negotiations were over.

He unleashed a trio of high-powered rounds, two of which tore into the man's side before he could fire back. The third destroyed his left kneecap.

Blood colored the man's silk shirt crimson. Despite the pain on his face, he tried to shoot back.

"Don't," Bolan warned.

Stubbornly he kept trying.

There wasn't time for pity. The Executioner let loose another short burst, this time at the man's face. His head exploded like an overripe melon.

The MAC-10 coughed three times in rapid succession as the second thug went for his gun, the 9 mm bone-crushers drilling holes in the gunner's throat, tearing open his carotid artery and exiting the other side.

As the suddenly dead assassin fell forward, the third one dived to the floor, reaching for his pistol as he did. Bolan made a half turn and chugged a lead triburst into his hand.

Bolan pointed the Ingram at the survivor, cringing under the table.

"On your feet," the soldier snapped in English.

The hardman pretended he didn't understand the order, his hand sliding to the Tokarev inside his waistband. Bolan fired a single round, aiming carefully so it tore a second hole in his palm.

"You'll live," Bolan promised, "if you start talking."

"I don't know anything," the man cried, clutching his

shattered palm with his other hand as he got to his feet and dropped into one of the chairs.

The thug kept looking at the blood spurting from the hole in his palm.

"I need a doctor."

"Where is Lushenska?"

The street fighter shook his head.

"Start talking or you'll need an undertaker."

"Kammil said he left for Brussels. That's all I know."

"Who's Kammil?"

The hood pointed to one of the dead men.

"He was one of the Russian's right hand men."

"When did the Russian leave?"

"Today. With a blond woman and another man."

"Did she have a German accent?"

The thug shrugged. Bolan repeated the question, pointing the Ingram at the shattered hand.

"Yes, she had a German accent," he said quickly.

It was starting to come together, but Bolan hadn't yet figured out who was planning to do what.

"Who was the man?"

"I don't know. An American."

"Describe him."

"I saw him only for a moment." He looked at his hand. "Please call a doctor. I will bleed to death."

"After you describe the man."

"He was tall and gray haired and very stuffy, like he thought he was very important."

For a moment the soldier wondered if the man was Rudy Johnson. It sounded just like him. Then he decided he'd find out soon enough.

By reputation, Lushenska liked to set up the missions, not play the assassin game personally. Who had he found to do the wet work—the blond German woman?

Lushenska was a Russian. From what he remembered

about Russian males, women hadn't yet achieved true equality, not even as assassins.

It had to be a man, but who? The gray-haired, stuffy man? Rudy Johnson?

Bolan knew he would have to search for the answer in Brussels.

He picked up the telephone on the desk and punched a series of numbers that would pass his call through a series of cutouts and finally connect him to Stony Man Farm. He had to let Brognola know he was heading to Brussels to search for the assassin. The message would be forwarded to the big Fed no matter where he was. Even if he was with the President.

23

Mack Bolan landed at Zaventem International Airport just before five. His canvas bags had been flown to Brussels on one of the government jets that crisscrossed Europe with confidential files and boxes of American-made equipment and supplies destined for embassies.

A courier from the American Embassy was waiting for him at the curb. The passport that identified Bolan as Mike Belasko satisfied the government messenger, who whispered an address and pointed to a new BMW 325i parked across the roadway.

Handing Bolan an envelope and the keys to the car and safehouse, the courier vanished onto a bus that carried airline passengers into the heart of Brussels.

The soldier dropped his bags on the floor beside him, started the small, powerful engine, then pulled out of the parking space and moved with the evening-rush-hour traffic toward the city.

A SMALL, UNKEMPT-LOOKING man got out of an ancient Renault and walked over to where four men were sitting in a Volvo. Wearing a soiled patterned shirt with frayed cuffs and collar, the little man reeked of sweat.

Looking nervously around to check if anybody was watching him, he leaned into the driver's window and gave the orders.

"Follow the BMW. The man driving it is the man in the

photograph the client sent me by fax," Sidney Marin said. "My contacts say he is probably going to this address." He handed the driver a handwritten note.

As the man walked back to his own car, got in and drove away, the gunmen in the Volvo remained expressionless. But one of the pair seated in the rear slipped an Israeli-made 9 mm parabellum Jericho semiautomatic pistol from his waistband and checked to make sure the magazine was full.

The hard-faced mercenary in the front passenger seat turned to the driver. "When do we make our move?"

The driver checked the address he'd just been given. He knew the place from prior missions.

"According to Marin, the Americans maintain a safe-house on the Rue de Portier in the Quartier des Marolles. That is where he will probably spend the night," the driver replied.

None of the men liked the small man who drove away from the airport. There was something snakelike about his expressions and attitude. But Sidney Marin was "the Contractor," one of the most important sources in Brussels for assignments like this.

Killing.

"The Contractor has hired a team to wait at the house and get rid of the man in case we get tied up in traffic."

One of the men in the back seat asked, "I wonder why this man is in Brussels?"

"Does it matter?" his back-seat companion asked.

"Exactly," the driver agreed. "We are being paid—well, I might remind all of you—to make sure he is not alive tomorrow."

The interior of the Volvo became silent as the foursome stared ahead at the BMW and their target, gripping their high-powered weapons in their hands.

ALWAYS ON THE ALERT for possible assailants, Bolan looked in the rearview mirror of the BMW. There was a Volvo right behind him, and it had been with him since he left the airport. The soldier wondered when the car was going to turn off the boulevard. Or were they following him?

Some sixth sense said they were.

He decided to slow down and see if the Volvo passed him. But the Swedish-made car maintained its distance.

Through the rearview mirror he could make out the faces of two men in the front seat of the Volvo. Turning his head quickly, he could see the hazy shapes of two more men sitting in the back.

The Executioner wondered who the four were.

The only thing he was sure of was that they had the cold, expressionless look of professionals.

Reaching down, he opened one of the two canvas carryalls containing the weapons and ammo the courier had brought through Belgian customs.

The 9 mm Beretta 93-R, and its shoulder holster, sat on top. Bolan picked it up and checked the magazine, which was full. He placed the pistol and holster on the seat next to him. He could see the mammoth .44 Magnum Desert Eagle and the mini-Uzi, but traffic was too heavy to risk an accident while trying to retrieve them.

The Beretta went into his waistband for the moment, and its holster back into the canvas bag.

It might all just be his overactive imagination, he reminded himself, and there was one way to find out. He checked the road ahead of him.

Leaning forward, he pushed down hard on the gas pedal. The car surged forward, and he swerved around the Fiat in front of him. Glancing in the side mirror, Bolan saw the large dark vehicle duplicating his maneuver.

Now he knew. He was the target.

He could slam on the brakes, jump out and try to eliminate the men following him, but there was always the chance that a stray slug would hit an innocent driver. The risk was too great. He'd have to outrun them.

Bolan could hear the protesting squeal of tires behind him as the other driver tried to keep up with his erratic bursts of speed.

He glanced in his rearview mirror and saw a flash of reflected sunlight bouncing off a metal object being held out of the front window of the car behind him.

He couldn't make out what kind of gun it was, and it didn't matter. At that range any pistol or subgun could take him out.

Over the rush of wind slamming against his car, he could hear the soft thud of slugs glancing off his vehicle. The chunks of hot lead pierced the skin of his vehicle as he kept trying to present as small a profile as he could to them. Before he was done with it, the embassy would be getting back a vehicle, scarred by searing lead slugs.

That was the least of his concerns. He'd let Brognola work out a settlement with embassy officials. Right now he was too busy trying to stay alive.

Bolan decided to try another tactic. He jammed down on the brakes. The Volvo almost slammed into his rear, then swerved and moved up parallel to his window.

Steering with his left hand, the Executioner grabbed the Beretta from his waistband with his right and aimed through his opened window at the other vehicle. As he emptied half the magazine, he saw the man framed in the Volvo's window drop his automatic pistol and grab for his face, then heard him shriek at the sudden pain.

Bolan couldn't risk an accident by taking his eyes off the road. Using instinct, he rapidly pumped two more rounds at the sound of the screaming man.

He heard the plinking sound of brass casing bouncing

against his door and the high-pitched whine as one of the hot lead slugs ricocheted.

As the soldier risked glancing at the other car briefly, he saw the man in the front passenger seat slide out of view.

The driver, an angry-looking man with a scar traversing his thick, jowled face, raised a squat, ugly automatic pistol and started to fire wildly at him. Bolan returned the fire and saw the driver grab his right shoulder. Then he heard the ominous metallic click as the Beretta's hammer hit metal.

There was no time to drop the magazine and snap in a new one. All he could do was try to outrun the other car.

He felt a burning tail of hot lead rush past his face as he pushed his head against the rest on his seat, then heard the ringing sound of two 9 mm parabellum slugs. They flew through the open window and hit the narrow metal trim around the driver's side window.

He had to take a chance.

Reaching down, he rummaged in the carryall for the Uzi submachine gun, then poked it out the window and fired three rounds back at the Volvo.

Quickly glancing over his shoulder, he saw the driver of the luxury vehicle slump forward, as if he had just decided he needed to take a nap. The driverless car started to swerve out of control.

One of the thugs in the rear threw himself forward and tried to grab the steering wheel, but it was too late. Like an enraged elephant, the Volvo went berserk, grazing the rear end of a Volkswagen sedan, then shoving a taxicab aside as it twisted its way in a figure-eight motion across the road, narrowly missing a station wagon coming in the opposite direction.

As the soldier slowed and watched, the metal behemoth crashed at full speed into a metal lamppost on the edge of the road and stopped momentarily. Suddenly the gas tank ruptured and exploded into a brilliant display of petrochemical fireworks.

A body flew through the metal framework that had once held a front windshield and rolled across the highway, stopping a few feet from the BMW.

Bolan shoved open his door and got out. He nudged the body with a toe, aiming his Uzi at it in case the gunman was still a threat.

Satisfied the gunman wasn't alive, he knelt and turned him over. What remained of the face was covered with blood-soaked dirt. Much of the neck had been shot away.

He looked at the overturned car and saw the other bodies trapped inside the twisted metal. He felt no regret. Killing was an ugly but necessary part of his job. He didn't have to like doing it, but on the path he had chosen, often it was a case of kill or be killed.

He heard sirens coming closer. Someone had stopped his car and gotten out.

"Do you understand English?" Bolan asked.

"A little," the man replied.

"I'm going to find a telephone and make sure they send an ambulance," Bolan told him.

"Good idea."

"You stay here and tell the police how these gangsters tried to kidnap me."

The French-speaking driver nodded. "So that's what these criminals were trying to do." He looked at the Uzi in Bolan's hand. "Is that one of their weapons?"

Bolan didn't want to arouse any more suspicions than necessary.

"Yes. I'm going to take it with me in case they have friends waiting to ambush me on the road. Then I'll turn it over to the police."

"Good idea," the Belgian agreed.

The soldier got in the BMW and drove away before the police arrived and detained him for questioning.

He had to find out who had sent the assassins.

And why.

As Lushenska and Schindler left the airport, the woman turned to the Russian.

"The American is still arguing with customs. I suppose we should wait," she said.

"It would be wise," Lushenska replied.

"I still don't know how you were able to get the weapons past customs."

"Friends from the past. And money," he answered.

She shook her head in amazement. Lushenska was somebody worth admiring. Unlike Marius, he was both tough *and* clever.

They got to the curb, where Johnson finally joined them.

"I want you two to take separate cabs to the Legend Hotel, on Rue de l'Etuve. It's an old-fashioned hotel, but very comfortable. While you were going through customs, I called them twice and made individual reservations," the Russian said, handing the woman a thick wad of bills.

"Aren't you going to stay there?"

"There are some things that need my personal attention." He smiled. "I would suggest that the two of you check in separately. No purpose in arousing suspicions about your relationship after tomorrow's event."

He turned to the American. "You do carry credit cards, don't you?"

"Of course."

"Use them. I'll reimburse you in Geneva."

He signaled two taxicabs to pull forward. Johnson picked up his bags and got into the first one. Lushenska waited until the cab had pulled away, then turned to Schindler.

"You might want to look at the quaint statue across the

street from the hotel. It's quite famous,'' he added with a smile.

He watched the cab disappear down the roadway, then turned and walked back into the terminal to a row of pay telephones. He walked to the farthest one and dialed the operator.

"I wish to place a collect call to Geneva."

ZELNICK HAD JUST finished dinner when he heard the telephone ring. His wife answered it.

"Someone calling collect for you, Hans," she announced, poking her head into the dining room.

"Did you get his name?"

"He said it was personal."

Zelnick went into the den and lifted the phone on his desk. He could hear his wife breathing into it.

"Hang up the telephone, Hilda," he said, irritated at her eavesdropping. He could hear her snort in anger as she finally complied. Then he told the operator he'd accept the call.

"Mr. Zelnick?"

"Yes, this is Zelnick. Who is this?"

"A friend in Brussels," was the reply.

Lushenska was calling him. For a moment the banker thought something was wrong.

"Is there a problem?"

"On the contrary. Everything is moving along on schedule. I am returning tonight. We need to meet."

"Can't it wait until the morning?"

"No. I'll be arriving in two hours. I'll wait in my car—a Volvo—in front of your offices until you arrive."

Before the banker could protest, the Russian hung up.

LUSHENSKA CHECKED his wristwatch. The Legend Hotel was a short drive from the airport. Johnson and Schindler should have arrived by now. He checked the telephone book and dialed the number for the hotel.

Margaritta Schindler was in her room.

"I must fly back to Geneva tonight. But I will return in the morning," he announced.

"What about the plan?"

"Call the American's room and tell him that you and I will meet him at the airport after the President is dealt with," the Russian said.

The woman sounded confused. "But you told me—"

"This is an open line," Lushenska warned. "But I think I may have eliminated possible interference from the man whose picture was in my desk drawer."

When Lushenska had called him from Geneva, the slimy little Belgian whose services he had retained in the past had guaranteed he would get rid of the man who called himself Belasko before morning.

"Tomorrow you will meet me at the KLM check-in counter at 2:00 p.m." The Russian paused. "Alone, I presume."

"I was hoping we could have dinner together."

"Tomorrow. Tonight I suggest you take a cab and survey the area outside the NATO building tonight. Find a place with enough height so that the rifle you acquired can reach past the crowds who will certainly gather."

"Do you mind if I invite some old friends to help?"

"Who?" Lushenska sounded tense.

"Three men who were on my team in the old days."

"How expensive?"

"I'll take care of them out of my share."

"Do they know for whom you work?"

"It wouldn't matter. They just miss the old days."

Lushenska relaxed. "I'll leave those decisions in your hands. You seem to know what you are doing."

"One more thing," the German woman said, laughing.

"You should have warned me that the statue across from the hotel was that of a little boy urinating."

"That is why they call it the Mannekin Pis," the Russian commented, joining in the laughter. "I hope things go easy."

"I've handled more-difficult assignments for Baader-Meinhof in the past."

"And not as profitable. Your share of the assignment will come to more than four hundred thousand, U.S."

Sounding gleeful, Schindler warned the Russian, "Now you've made it difficult for me to sleep, trying to decide what to do with all that money."

"It's only the beginning, my dear," Lushenska promised, and hung up to catch his flight to Geneva.

24

Sitting behind the wheel, Andres was grateful for the lack of moonlight. It made it possible for the former soldier of fortune to keep an eye on the American safehouse at the edge of the Marolles district until the target arrived.

He could see shaded lights inside the tiny brick house, but he had seen a small, elderly cleaning woman leave them on when she left the structure an hour ago.

He checked his wristwatch while he waited for the other car to join him. It was almost midnight. He hoped the man he had been hired to eliminate would show up soon so he could get back to his apartment and get some sleep.

A car drove by slowly and stopped next to him. It was Louis, one of the men he had hired for the hit.

He looked at the stout, bearded man behind the wheel and the other three men with him.

"Any sign of the American?"

The man behind the wheel of the second car shook his head, then asked, "Are you sure this is where he will come?"

"According to the Contractor, this is where he will spend the night," Andres replied.

"But what if the men at the airport have already taken care of him?"

Andres held up a cellular phone. "The Contractor just called. There was a news report on the radio. The men at the airport were in an accident while pursuing him."

Like many of the professional killers in Brussels, Andres got most of his assignments from Sidney Marin, who operated an all-night coffee shop in the slum district of the city as a cover.

The professional leaned his head out of his car. "Take the others and watch the front. And let's make sure we don't miss him."

"Who is this man?"

Andres shook his head. "I don't know. Or care. We are being paid for making sure he dies. And paid a hell of a lot more money than we got when we were fighting in the Congo."

Andres and the other four men had worked as a team for many years. Mercenaries in Africa, they had turned to accepting assignments to kill when Belgium abandoned its claims on its former colony.

Work didn't come as frequently as it used to during the Cold War. But fortunately for them, Marin's assignments paid well enough so they could survive until the next one came along.

"Someone should stand guard at the back door until he shows up," Andres ordered, then decided to do it himself.

He got out of his car and opened the trunk. From an aluminum suitcase, he took out a stubby 9 mm Uzi machine pistol and several full magazines.

He glanced at the side arms the men in the second car wore in their leather holsters. "Is that the heaviest artillery you men have?"

All four reached down to the floor and brought into view the SMGs they had placed there.

Andres looked pleased. "The client says this guy's the best fighter the Americans have. He has to be put out of business tonight."

The others shrugged. "We've heard that about every gunfighter who comes to Brussels," Louis commented.

"There's a nice bonus in it if we take him out," Andres added.

Mention of the additional reward brought a smile to the faces of the four men.

THE EXECUTIONER had parked the scarred BMW around the corner and watched the men in the two cars as they held a brief conference. Somebody was trying to make sure he couldn't stop the assassination attempt.

With Alexander Marius dead, he was sure he knew who had hired them—Viktor Lushenska.

But he was puzzled. The Russian was a professional. With his client gone, why would he want to continue the assignment?

Unless Lushenska hadn't heard about the battle in Courchevel.

Bolan was positive he had.

There were only two reasons for the Russian to continue the assignment: his pride at always finishing a job, or someone else had hired him.

From his experience, the soldier knew that most professional killers had no pride. They did what they did because they were getting paid for it.

But there was a real possibility somebody else was taking over the arms syndicate. Bolan couldn't imagine who. All of the other partners had been killed in the shoot-out.

Then he remembered that the Swiss banker hadn't been present, or had left before the warrior had arrived.

The Executioner decided Hans Zelnick deserved a personal visit. But it would have to wait until after the President's arrival at NATO to address the council.

Right now he had to take care of the hit men so he could get some sleep. He started to develop a strategy in his mind. There were two cars. One had only a driver, who Bolan assumed was in charge of the attack. The other vehicle was carrying four hitters.

The car parked near the rear entrance contained the leader, so Bolan decided to take care of him first.

Digging through his canvas carryall, he extracted two frag grenades, he got out of the BMW and worked his way in the shadows to the corner where the alley and rear driveway met. Then he pulled the pin on the first grenade and carefully rolled the bomb under the killer's vehicle.

Ducking back behind the building, Bolan waited.

The explosion flung chunks of torn metal in every direction. Gasoline sprayed from the ruptured tank and soaked the rear driveway.

There was one last thing the soldier had to do. Picking up a discarded copy of a newspaper, he twisted the paper together, took a lighter from one of his pockets and lit one end of the makeshift torch.

Tossing it at the remnants of the car, Bolan pulled back into the alley and waited. A wave of gasoline-fumed flames whooshed into being, engulfing the wrecked vehicle.

The trapped driver screamed in agony as the flames consumed his flesh. Bolan showed mercy to the agonized man, delivering one precise round to his head. Then there was silence.

The Executioner knew the others wouldn't wait long to see what had happened. Reaching into his car, he retrieved the Uzi SMG and a handful of magazines, flattened himself against the wall of the building and waited.

Five minutes passed. From the street he could hear an engine start. The sound of a car grew louder, and the other waiting gunmen pulled into the alley.

Curses were emitted when the driver saw that the narrow road was blocked by the BMW.

Bolan watched the front and rear doors open and four

heavily armed thugs get out. The battle had come down to four to one.

The soldier waited for the quartet to huddle, then separate.

One of the mercenaries held a large flashlight in one hand and a 9 mm Browning Hi-Power in the other. As Bolan watched, the thug illuminated the ground and walls. He knew that in a minute or two, the hired gun would find his hiding place. It was time to act.

Slipping the Applegate-Fairbairn blade from its sheath, the Executioner waited until the hunter started to pass him, then clamped his left hand over the shooter's mouth and swiftly ran the razor-sharp blade across the mercenary's throat.

A thin, clean slash began to slowly exhale blood as the vessels in the throat separated. Bolan held the would-be killer tightly until he saw the crimson fluid begin to gush down the hit man's chest.

The hardman tried to hold his head up, but finally surrendered and let it slump forward as he died.

The Executioner eased the body to the ground and pulled it against the brick wall of the house. One down, three to go.

The Executioner could hear the three remaining hitters as they headed in his direction. No more clandestine moves. He'd have to confront them openly.

Grasping his Uzi, he set the fire-selector switch to continuous fire and waited for the three men to come closer.

All three were gripping H&K MP-5 subguns. The German submachine gun was one of the most accurate multiple-fire weapons available, and Bolan had a great deal of respect for its power.

As if they were soldiers on close-drill parade, the three men moved slowly in his direction. They kept scanning the area, looking for his hiding place.

The soldier decided it was time to stop playing cat and mouse. He stepped out into the open, his Uzi held tightly at his side.

There was no exchange of words, just bullets flashing from the Uzi and the MP-5s. The soldier's rounds found their intended targets, chewing into breastbones and midsections.

Bolan washed the trio with a spray of hollowpoint lead, but not before one of them fired back. One of the rounds tore into the Executioner's upper left arm.

He could feel the burning as the hard ball carved an entry hole in his arm and exited, chewing into the brick wall behind him.

One of the three attackers spun at the impact of the Executioner's lead, then dropped his SMG and fell to the ground, facing in the opposite direction.

A second sneered at Bolan and tried to raise his weapon for a second attempt, then showed his surprise when his fingers wouldn't obey the command he thought his brain was sending them.

Still wearing an expression of astonishment on his face, he crumpled to the ground in a pool of his own blood and gore.

The final hitter stared in shock at his fallen partners, then started to raise his hands in surrender, only to discover he was too late. He was already dead, as he found out when his legs turned to rubber and his body scraped against the dirt and crushed rocks that covered the floor of the alley.

Bolan checked the bodies before he gave any thought to the burning in his left arm. It was part of the routine. The part that had kept him from becoming a victim of a supposedly dead killer.

Satisfied the four were dead, he moved past the burned wreckage of the car and hurried to the safehouse. Using the key to enter the building, Bolan turned on the lights and found himself in a small kitchen. He walked through the door in the opposite wall and down a small corridor until he reached a living room. A medical kit rested on a dining table. He opened it and found bandages and antibiotics inside. Stripping off his shirt, he dressed the wound, then went outside and retrieved the two bags from the BMW.

Setting them down in the living room, he saw a long, rigid plastic case and a soft leather case.

He opened the leather bag first, which held a pair of powerful binoculars—Zeiss 10×30s.

In the bag, he also found a small transmitter with a built-in microphone and an earpiece.

There were latches on the plastic case. He snapped them open and looked inside. A long-barreled weapon nestled in cushioned foam. It was a Stoner SR-25, the same gun that had killed the pair of assassins in Porto Santos. Several 20-round magazines of high-powered 168-grain .308 ammo were tucked into the foam, and a note.

You can reach me at the American Embassy tonight. Use the portable set to maintain contact after the President starts his journey to the NATO headquarters.

There was no signature. None was needed. Bolan knew that Hal Brognola had sent the equipment.

BOLAN PICKED UP the telephone and asked the operator for the American Embassy's number, then dialed it and asked for the big Fed.

"Brognola," the voice on the other end answered.

"Thanks for the presents," Bolan said.

"I just got a report from Belgian Intelligence that you had some visitors at your house."

"Five. They're dead."

"I know. It took some hard convincing by the ambassador to stop the police from investigating the shooting."

"What about the bodies?"

"Get some sleep. You've got a busy day ahead of you. We sent some men to haul them and the auto wreck away." He paused. "Any damage?"

"A few scratches."

"That's what the first-aid kit is for. I'll have someone look at you tomorrow. After the President leaves."

"How's the President getting to the NATO building?"

"He took your suggestion and had an armored limousine flown over to drive him there."

"The Secret Service made the same suggestion," Bolan reminded Brognola.

"I guess neither one of you wants to see the President killed. The problem is he'll want to walk the last hundred yards on foot. And no matter how many guards protect him, he's going to want to shake a lot of hands."

"I'll be there in case the wrong types show up."

"Pick a location?"

"I will before tomorrow. See you then."

25

It was almost two in the morning when Margaritta Schindler made the last call, then decided to take a bath. Franz would be picking her up outside the hotel in an hour.

Looking much older than he had the last time she saw him, the slender man waited for her to come out of the front door of the hotel, then embraced her.

She was carrying a long case, which he took from her.

"You are as beautiful as ever," he said.

"And you, Franz, are still the best liar we ever had," she replied with a grin.

"I am amazed that you still keep tabs on us after all these years. How did you know we live in Brussels?"

"That is not important," she answered, then looked at the Scandinavian-made car. "Is this yours?"

Nodding, Franz opened the passenger door of the Saab. Schindler got in and let him close it. He set the case down on the rear seat and got in behind the wheel.

"You reached the others?" the woman asked.

"Yes. They are excited at the prospect of working with you again. So am I."

Schindler knew more about what her three ex-compatriots had been doing since their Baader-Meinhof Gang days than the man behind the wheel realized.

Escaping from Germany, the trio had stuck together and buried themselves in the slums of Brussels. Somehow they had acquired false identities and passports. She knew they had barely survived over the years by taking on temporary assignments for radical movements in Europe and the Middle East.

"Where are we meeting Willem and Carl?"

"At the most logical place. Outside the NATO building."

"You always were the logical one, Franz," she said, then leaned her head back against the seat and stared out of the front windshield.

The Saab moved along the Rue de l'Etuve, working its way through the hordes of tourists crowded around the statue of the uninhibited child, and increased its speed as it reached the wide boulevards.

At a swift pace the driver moved across the city until he reached Avenue Leopold and drove around the huge, curved structure down a side road and stopped.

"And we are here," Franz announced, "in record time." He then got out and opened the door for her.

He started to lead her along a wide walkway when he saw her stop.

"The case," she reminded him.

Looking embarrassed, Franz opened the rear door and picked up the case. Then he led the way.

A wide plaza faced the rows of flags in front of the building. Each was the national flag of a member country.

Margaritta Schindler turned her back on them and stared at the open spaces in front of her. There were only a few places to hide.

She spotted the Television Europe truck. Parked at one side of the plaza, the vehicle was multileveled, and built on top of the roof of the heavy van was a superstructure.

The blonde knew it had been built to allow a cameraman to get high enough above the crowds to focus on celebrities arriving at the building. She had seen similar trucks before, covering major events.

It was the perfect location for a cameraman and an assassin, as she had told Franz when she contacted him.

A man wearing a jacket with the logo of Television Europe on his left breast smiled as she approached. Schindler smiled in turn.

"When did you start working for a television network, Willem?"

The tall gray-haired man grinned broadly and lifted her in his arms, then set her down. "Actually I was a television cameraman for a while," he said proudly, "when one of the cells of the Red Brigades wanted someone to record one of their kidnappings." He shook his head. "Those Italians always want to show off to one another."

"Where's Carl?"

A stocky man came from behind the television truck, wiping blood from a large knife with a rag. Like Willem, he wore a Television Europe jacket.

"Like always I was too busy cleaning up a mess to just hang around and hug you," he growled, glaring at the lanky man.

Schindler kissed the heavyset man on the cheek.

"And the crew of this unit?"

Carl turned to Franz. "Is there room in your trunk for them?"

Franz nodded.

"Then come and help."

The two men disappeared around the truck and began to carry a large plastic bag to the rear of the Saab. One of them opened the trunk, and the pair shoved the bag inside, then vanished and returned with a second plastic bag, then a third and a fourth.

Franz got in behind the steering wheel. The stocky man got in beside him and opened his window to look at Schindler.

"I need a picture of you," Carl said.

"I don't have one."

"No problem," Franz replied, and picked up a Polaroid camera from the floor of the van. "The driver must have been impatient. Obviously he wanted to see the photographs he had taken immediately."

He handed her a Television Europe baseball cap.

"Put this on and pull it down over your eyes."

Schindler did.

Franz aimed the instant camera, took several pictures and handed the results to the man still holding the combat knife.

"We'll be back as soon as we get rid of this garbage, and make some alterations to the identity cards they were carrying," the heavyset man growled.

Schindler watched the small car that had been parked behind the van drive away.

When they were alone, Willem looked at the case the woman was carrying. "It looks like you're ready."

"As soon as I put this together," she answered.

Getting into the truck, she flipped open the latches and lifted the top. The components of the unassembled 7.62 mm M-82 Parker-Hale sniper's rifle fit neatly in the foam compartments of the transit case. A wide-angle scope, ready to be mounted on the British-made weapon, sat in its own foam indent. Three full 4-round magazines were snugly fitted in a foam pocket next to them.

Giving the task her full concentration, Schindler assembled the powerful weapon. From previous experience she knew the rifle was designed to give one hundred percent first-round-hit capability at up to 400 meters.

The suppressor eliminated all muzzle-flash and reduced recoil without affecting distance or accuracy. The night-vision sight and a matching daytime telescope sight eliminated the need for open sights.

Each part fit perfectly, and within twenty minutes the blond woman had the weapon completely assembled. Testing the trigger action, she found the movement light and smooth.

Sighting the night-vision device and the scope took time, requiring the woman to make minute adjustments again and again.

Finally she raised the rifle to her shoulder and focused on the steps that led up to the main entrance. She checked the gauge on the scope. The distance was 350 meters.

Satisfied, she snapped one of the magazines into the weapon and pushed the first round into the chamber, then climbed the steps to the upper platform of the van and hid the weapon under a tarpaulin.

Now she was ready, and anxious for morning to come.

Climbing down the steps, she knew that Willem had watched her work without saying a word. She turned her head and looked at him. His expression was one of admiration.

"You are like an artist," he commented.

"Like anything else one does well, this is an art," she acknowledged.

"Do we have uniforms to wear?"

He nodded and handed her a pair of dark pants, a jacket embroidered with the network's name and logo. She already had a baseball cap bearing the station's logo.

The woman slipped into the small sedan parked behind the van. Without modesty, she stripped down to her bra and panties, and slipped into the garments one of the dead network employees had worn. She hid her dress and jacket under the front seat.

Opening her purse, she took out the loaded Walther PPK and slipped it into one of the jacket pockets, then slid the handbag under the seat, next to her clothing.

"What time does our man arrive?"

Willem opened the local newspaper and snapped on the interior light.

"According to the printed schedule, he will drive from the American Embassy and be here at ten."

Schindler looked at the tiny watch on her wrist.

"Seven hours." She sighed.

There was no reason to return to the hotel. She'd sleep in the van.

"Wake me when it's eight," she ordered, then closed her eyes and, feeling no tension to interfere with her rest, fell promptly asleep.

26

Bolan couldn't sleep. Strange dreams kept creeping into his mind, keeping him awake. Lushenska's face smirked at him and dared him to find the Russian before he killed the President. The blond German woman was standing next to the Russian mocking the warrior. Finally Bolan climbed out of bed and dressed.

At least he could check the area where the President would walk on his way to address the NATO council.

The Beretta 93-R went into the shoulder holster he slipped on, while the .44 Magnum Desert Eagle was tucked into the rigid case mounted on his heavy leather belt. There was no need for the SMGs, not tonight.

He peered through a window. Nobody seemed to be watching the safehouse. Stepping outside, he got into the BMW and decided to check out the more public places in Brussels.

Even at this late hour, the area around the colossal structure known as the Palais de Justice was filled with protesters: African Americans were holding posters high denouncing the injustices committed in what used to be the Belgian Congo, and also protested the fact that American tourists still visited Belgium; Iranian students and young men and women of Jewish extraction from the nearby slum area called the Marolles kept clashing, separated only by Belgian riot police; local protest groups railed loudly at one another, and blamed the Americans for allowing NATO to continue operating in Brussels.

Bolan knew better. After Charles de Gaulle, one-time war hero and later president of France, had demanded that NATO withdraw from his country, Belgium had welcomed the North Atlantic Treaty Organization members and offered them a new home.

As the soldier stopped and watched from his car, he could see tempers begin to flare. Police, holding shields in front and using batons to drive protesters from the square, tried to keep peace.

It was a good reminder to Bolan that hired assassins weren't the only force that wanted to see the American President dead. There were terrorist groups from a great number of countries who advocated the murder of the American leader.

Saddened by the violence, the warrior started the engine. It was time to have a personal look at the proposed killing field, the plaza in front of the NATO headquarters building.

Checking his weapons, he decided it might be smart to bring along something heavier.

He drove around a corner and headed back to the safehouse.

THE RADIO WAS BLARING the news about the sudden violence in Brussels: first the shoot-out at the airport, then the pair of exploding cars in the Marolles district.

For Sidney Marin, the violence was getting too close for comfort. If he couldn't find some men who could eliminate the American mercenary, the violence would be inside his small restaurant.

And he would be in the middle of it.

He hadn't called the client in Geneva to tell him the bad news. Already the mistakes of the dead men had cost him almost all the profit he had hoped to make on this assignment. If he didn't find a group to carry out the job, the mistakes might cost him his own life.

Business had been good until tonight. Hate between the various ethnic groups always ended with his getting new clients, recommended by clients who were satisfied with the work he had done for them.

But not this night.

He wondered who was available, then looked up and saw three unshaved men enter his empty coffee shop. He knew them. Until they turned to drugs for their recreation, the three Breton brothers were among the best shooters in Brussels.

Studying them, he knew they had been splurging on narcotics. It didn't matter what kinds of drugs they had used. Drugs and professionals didn't mix, but Marin was desperate.

The three sat at the counter.

"Coffee," one of the men shouted.

"On the house," Marin replied as he served demitasse cups of a thick black brew.

He leaned an elbow on the counter and smiled at them. "Looks like the three of you have had a successful night."

The trio looked at one another and shook their heads.

"Successful? Would you believe some asshole drug dealer wouldn't give us credit?"

The restaurant owner feigned surprise. "Really?"

One of the three grabbed Marin by the collar and pulled him forward. "Know anybody who could use our services?"

The coffee shop owner held up his hands. "Maybe. If you're not too expensive."

"Right now," the second man growled, "we'd be willing to work for anything reasonable."

Marin decided sharing too much information would get in their way. He thought quickly and invented a situation. "I got a call from a man who occasionally uses my services."

Jules Breton, the spokesman of the brothers, sounded impatient. "Who does he want killed?"

"Well, there is a man who has gotten a little too important. He's making this client's life hell. The man thinks that just because he's big and good with a gun, he can do anything he wants. Actually he's a poor shot and a coward."

He let the words sink in while the three drug-hungry brothers looked at one another with grins.

"I should warn you that the man is an American. He works for the American Embassy as a troubleshooter."

"I don't care if he works for God," Jules growled. "How much?"

Marin quickly added up his costs until now. He decided he would try to keep losses to a minimum as he named a fee.

"Pretty small fee," one of the other brothers snarled.

"I could probably talk him into going up another ten percent," the coffee shop owner murmured.

"Better," the third shooter said. The other two nodded their agreement.

"When do we get paid?" Jules asked.

"As soon as the radio announces his death."

Before they could change their minds, Marin scribbled an address on a paper napkin and handed it to them.

"He's staying here tonight."

The three street fighters got off their seats, then turned to the coffee shop owner.

"We'll be back later. Just have the money ready," Jules stated.

THREE GRUBBY-LOOKING men were leaning against a small battered car as Bolan drove onto the street. At first he thought they were among the many who were homeless, then saw the long raincoats they were wearing, and the telltale bulges beneath them. Studying their expressions, he knew them for what they were—hit men.

Bolan decided to let them make the first move, just in case he was wrong about them. Ignoring the trio, he drove down the narrow alley and parked behind the safehouse.

JULES BRETON took charge of the assault. He pointed to the two ends of the small house and whispered, "Each of you go to one of the sides. I'll go in the front to drive him out."

"What if he refuses to come out?" his younger brother asked.

He dug deep into his raincoat pocket and brought out an incendiary grenade.

"Then I'll burn him out," he boasted.

"Good thinking. And when he comes out, we fire."

"Right," Jules replied.

The three hit men withdrew the submachine guns they had hidden under their raincoats. Jules put the grenade back into his pocket so he could get a steadier grip on his 9 mm TEC-9.

The other two waited for his signal, then fanned out and moved toward the house.

BOLAN WATCHED through a window as the tallest of the three approached the front door. The other two, he was certain, were going to try to get him by breaking into the house through the rear door and one of the side windows.

Bolan had grown weary of the attacks on him since his arrival. He had wanted to keep his mind focused on the reason he was in Brussels, to protect the life of the President, not duel with three hit men.

Unlocking the front door, he pulled the entrance wide open.

The crude-looking thug who stood on the outside steps was caught off guard. Raising the TEC-9 in his hands, the Belgian jerked his finger back on the trigger, then looked surprised when the target suddenly wasn't standing in front of him, absorbing the lead from his subgun.

Bolan had thrown himself to the right of the open door. Lashing out a foot, he tripped the gunman. As he fell to the floor, the hired killer tightened his grip on his automatic weapon and started to hose the living room with lead.

Three bullets from the Executioner's Uzi drilled into the blood vessels in the shooter's neck. Blood spurted from the shattered arteries and stained the wall vermilion. The hitter tried to fire the weapon in his hands, but his fingers wouldn't obey his brain's command.

Still staring at the big American who had gotten to his feet, the unshaved thug let his head fall forward and kissed the rug with dead lips.

Shattered glass got an immediate reaction from the Executioner, who dived to the floor and rolled to one side of the fractured window.

A hand reached in from outside, feeling for the lock that kept the frame closed. The soldier pushed himself up from the floor and rammed his right hand against the attacker's hand. A long shard of glass forced its way through the Belgian's wrist until it poked through on the other side.

Screams from outside permeated the room as the gunman tried to pull his hand free of the glass dagger. Blood shot a fountain of dark red from the severed artery in the would-be killer's wrist.

For a brief moment the Executioner found compassion

for the shrieking Belgian. Aiming his Uzi at the lower half of the broken window, Bolan released a trio of rounds.

A loud grunt filled the living room as a body fell forward and was skewered on the shattered fragments of the glass window.

A volley of reverberating rounds tore into the door that led from the kitchen. A fragment nicked the soldier's upper left arm. Despite the sharp pain, Bolan moved to the wall next to the portal and pressed his body against the plaster.

A shoulder rammed the door and forced it open.

Behind the shoulder was a quivering hood, grasping a TEC-9 submachine gun.

Bolan waited until the assailant entered the living room, then fired his Uzi, watching as two rounds chugged into the attacker. Then metal clanged on metal. The soldier's weapon was empty.

Reaching for the Desert Eagle in the waistband holster, Bolan cleared leather and raised it into target acquisition.

Bleeding from the newly opened cavity in his chest and the hole in his left shoulder, the gunman stared at the gun in the Executioner's hand, then turned and fled out the back door.

Bolan started to chase after him, but decided to let him go. The man was badly wounded and knew that he was outgunned. He wouldn't be back.

Surveying the damage, Bolan lifted the phone on an end table and dialed the number Brognola had given him.

"Two more outside and one running down the street who probably won't make it," he reported.

"A team will be by soon to scrape them up and find the third guy," the big Fed promised. "Anything else?"

"I could use an M-67 launcher and a HEAT missile."

There was a sharp whistle on the other end of the line. "You trying to start World War III?"

"No, stop it if I can," the Executioner replied.

There was a pause, then, "Take a long drive. At least an hour," Brognola said. "The place will be relatively clean when you get back. And look in the bedroom closet. There'll be a launcher and a pair of HEAT rockets waiting for you."

27

Bolan loaded the BMW with his newly cleaned and reloaded weapons and worked his way across Brussels to the NATO administrative headquarters on the other side of the city. As he pulled to the empty curb, he gazed through the driver's window at the vast open space. The following day, thousands of men, women and children would crowd into the area, hoping to catch a glimpse of the President of the United States.

If he was lucky, that's all who would show up.

The Executioner knew it was only wishful thinking on his part.

Somewhere in Brussels there was a professional killer waiting for morning, when he or she could assassinate the President.

Unless Bolan could stop it.

He stepped out of the borrowed car and walked across the wide plaza. In the distance he could see a television truck already parked. Nobody seemed to be near it.

He decided to check and make sure.

A police officer walked up from behind and asked him to stop.

Slowly Bolan turned. His ID picture card clipped to his jacket identified Bolan as a special security agent for the President.

He had a second card clipped to the jacket, which had

been issued by the Belgian government. It permitted him to carry weapons and to go anyplace he wanted.

The uniformed cop studied the two cards, then looked apologetic.

"Sorry, *monsieur*. I have to check everybody who approaches this area before your President arrives here."

"Understood," Bolan replied, then pointed to the television van. "What about them?"

The officer glanced at the Television Europe truck.

"I've checked them several times. They cover every major event here and in other countries."

For some reason the policeman's answer didn't satisfy the Executioner. He decided it was the tension he was feeling about the safety of the President.

"Something bothering you?" asked a familiar voice.

Bolan turned to see Hal Brognola, in the company of a Belgian colonel.

"Yeah, but I don't see anything wrong. Chalk it up to paranoia, I guess."

"I'll take your paranoia over anybody else's gut instincts," the head of Stony Man Farm replied.

Brognola changed the subject. He pointed to the uniformed military man standing next to him.

"Colonel LaFonte is responsible for the safety of important foreign visitors. Anything you need or want he'll try to provide."

The thick-mustached colonel held out his hand, which Bolan shook.

"How can we be of assistance, Mr. Belasko?"

Bolan turned his head and studied the plaza. "Where can I stand and get a clear view of the President?"

The tall soldier rubbed his chin. "That is difficult. With the crowds the local police expect tomorrow, I'm afraid only those next to your President will be able to clearly see him.''

The answer gave the Executioner some feeling of relief. Secret Service agents, and Brognola, would be surrounding the President.

The colonel gave the question some more thought, then turned to the policeman.

In French, he asked, ''Do you still erect those tall platforms for better crowd control?''

''But of course,'' the man replied.

Turning to Bolan, the colonel made a suggestion. ''To maintain crowd control the police erect high stands that are connected by radio transmitters. So, if there is any trouble—or a hint of trouble—anywhere in the plaza, they can summon reinforcements to that place.''

''Can I get access to one of them, preferably one close to where the President will get out of his limousine?''

''I will arrange it,'' the colonel promised. ''May I ask why?''

''If there's trouble that could endanger the life of the President, I would like to be able to deal with it immediately.''

The Belgian soldier was about to protest, but Brognola took his arm and started to lead him away.

''I'll explain the situation in private,'' the big Fed said.

He stopped and turned back to Bolan. ''What are you doing here at this hour?''

''The same as you. Checking the killing field.''

Brognola shook his head in resignation. ''If I thought you'd take orders, I'd order you to go back to the house and rest. You're going to need everything you've got tomorrow morning.''

RUDY JOHNSON couldn't sleep. At first he blamed the ventilation in his hotel room.

Tossing and turning in the large bed, he kept remembering how his life had once been, before Mike Belasko had destroyed it: memories of a career of service, missions personally handled, missions he had led, missions he had conceived.

That life had come to a halt in the White House a few days earlier. Now he was part of the Central Intelligence Agency's past, retired with prejudice.

He picked up the ornate ring and the small vial of poison he had placed on the nightstand.

This was how the President would die. At least it would be swift and painless.

Perhaps if Belasko was in Brussels, he would take care of him next.

Placing the large ring and bottle back on the nightstand, the former deputy director of operations for the CIA closed his eyes and tried to shut out the confusion in his brain that was preventing him from sleeping.

FRANZ NUDGED Schindler's shoulder gently. She opened her eyes and stared at him.

"Is something wrong?"

"There's a policeman and an army colonel studying the area. They have two civilians with them."

Lifting her head slightly, she could see the four men. Three of them she didn't know. The fourth she would have recognized anyplace.

His build, his stance, the icy expression of his face, the dead eyes: Mike Belasko, the supposedly dead American mercenary.

Like Lushenska, she had a begrudging admiration for the man. He was a killer, like she was. The difference was she usually killed for a worthwhile cause. Except for the few years she had worked for the Union Corse chief.

According to what the Russian had told her, Belasko killed for the pleasure of killing, a brutal animal who needed to be destroyed. And would be, she promised herself, after she took care of the American President.

This wasn't the moment to make her companions nervous with the truth.

"Forget them," she said casually. "Just a bunch of cops playing bloodhounds."

Franz glanced out of his window. The four men were leaving.

"They're going," he reported.

"And now that they're done trying to act like Sherlock Holmes, they'll go home to their warm beds and brag about how they worked late to make sure the American visitor would be safe."

The other three in the van grinned at her wry humor as Schindler closed her eyes and let her head rest against the back of her seat.

28

Lushenska had picked up his Mercedes-Benz 500 SL sports car in the parking area of the Geneva airport and driven to Zelnick's bank. The front of the building had been still dark when he had gotten there. The Swiss banker hadn't arrived yet.

The Russian parked across the deserted street.

Finally an American Cadillac pulled up to the curb in front of the bank building. Zelnick got out and signaled the Russian to join him.

Looking around to make sure no one was watching, Lushenska crossed the street and joined Zelnick.

The elderly banker looked at the Russian. "What is so important it couldn't wait for tomorrow?"

"When we get inside," Lushenska insisted.

Zelnick led him around the corner and down a narrow walkway to a side door. He pressed a doorbell.

The elderly guard looked sour as he peered out of the thick glass door. Then changed his expression when he saw the Swiss banker. Quickly he opened the door.

"Herr Zelnick, what are you doing here so late?"

"An emergency meeting, Arnold," he said smoothly, and led Lushenska down a series of halls until they came to an ornate pair of doors.

"My personal office," Zelnick explained, opening the doors.

The Russian was impressed. The banker had done well for himself. The large room was filled with antiques. Even the rug was a Persian, which had to have been several hundred years old.

Zelnick saw him stare at it.

"When Iran was still Persia, this rug hung on the wall in one of the Shah's many throne rooms. I bought it from a representative of the current government who decided such ornate objects did not fit in with the way of life in his country. He wanted the money in a foreign bank just in case he decided to relocate."

Lushenska recognized some of the paintings hanging on the walls. As a lover of fine art, he had seen some of them in art books. Each had been captioned with the warning, "Stolen by the Nazis." Which, the Russian decided, was from whom Zelnick had bought them.

The Swiss banker saw his visitor study the decorations in his office.

"Do you like them?"

"I am very impressed," Lushenska admitted.

Zelnick took a seat behind the long hand-carved table that served as his desk. "Now, what was so important that I had to come here in the middle of the night?"

"I want to withdraw my money from your bank," the Russian said.

Zelnick looked shocked. "You cannot do that after regular banking hours."

"You mean the head of the bank cannot get into his own vaults?"

"Of course I can. But that's not how we do business."

"My people are waiting for a call from me about carrying out the assignment. If I don't call, they will pack their equipment and return home. As will the American President after he makes his speech."

"You can't do that," the banker shouted. "We have already paid you half your fee."

"No. The prior management did. And they are dead."

Zelnick shook his head. "A mere technicality. None of the men who served as directors of the arms companies owned any stock in them. Only my bank did. And I am the official representative of my bank."

Lushenska was amused. He was about to get another lesson in banking conniving.

"Who put up the money to buy these arms companies?"

"The organizations the directors represented. But all the stock was being held in a secret trust. The companies' records will show that the only stockholder was this bank."

"Very clever," the Russian admitted. "So now you take over and collect all the income."

"Not all," Zelnick said. "Those groups who were our customers will get a share of the profits."

"And that makes the bank the official owner."

"Exactly." He smiled. "Of course, we will need your assistance from time to time, when a competitor becomes too difficult to deal with on some other basis."

Lushenska reached into his pocket and wrapped his fingers around the Russian-made 7.62 mm pistol with its built-in silencer.

"So there is no point in killing the American President."

"On the contrary," Zelnick replied. "It is very important that he die so the demand for our products grows."

Lushenska stood. "Then I must also insist on being paid the rest of our fee."

"Nonsense," Zelnick snapped. "You will be paid when you complete the contract."

The Russian took out the pistol and pointed it at the banker. "On the contrary. I will be paid now. Or you will die."

Zelnick stared in horror at the weapon in Lushenska's hand.

"Be reasonable. Come back in the morning and we can settle this like businessmen."

He saw the determined expression on the other man's face.

"I can give you a part of the stock in the companies," he suggested.

The Russian shook his head. "I am a poor one for business. The only thing I know how to do is what I've been doing for most of my adult life. Killing people."

Zelnick started to argue, then closed his mouth. "Very well. If that is what you want, follow me."

The Russian slipped the weapon back in his coat pocket and eased his hand around it. He followed Zelnick down a series of halls until they stopped in front of a pair of thick steel doors.

Blocking Lushenska's view with his body, Zelnick turned the dials until a pair of loud clicks were heard, then pulled the doors open.

He turned to the Russian. "This is not our main vault. That is sealed by a time lock. This is my own vault for those times when some urgent business comes out that cannot wait for regular banking hours."

Lushenska understood. With the kinds of clients the other man laundered currency for, such a satellite vault was essential.

It was what he had expected to exist.

Following the banker inside, Lushenska watched as Zelnick counted out wrapped stacks of American currency and shoved them into several canvas sacks.

He could see Zelnick's hands tremble as he worked. Not, Lushenska decided, because the banker was afraid of the gun. But because he was giving money away, instead of receiving it.

Finally the banker was finished counting. Lushenska knew he had been cheated, but four million dollars was still a sizable sum.

Lifting the bags, he followed Zelnick out of the vault and watched while the banker closed them behind him.

"You go ahead," the banker suggested. "I have to fill out some forms."

"No. We will leave together."

Zelnick was about to argue, until he stared at the Russian's pocketed hand and saw it become stiffer. "Of course," he suddenly agreed.

"And you carry one of these sacks."

Reluctantly the banker hoisted the canvas bag and led the way to the side door.

The elderly guard was sitting there. He stood when he saw the two men. "Can I help you carry the bag, Herr Zelnick?"

"I am sure Mr. Zelnick would rather carry it himself," the Russian said.

The guard opened the door and let the two men out onto the small walkway.

"You can walk me to my car," Lushenska said, pointing to the Mercedes across the street.

The banker reluctantly walked across the wide roadway and waited at the trunk while the Russian opened it.

"Put it inside," Lushenska ordered.

He could see the tears start to form in Zelnick's eyes as the man lifted the heavy sack and dropped it inside the luggage compartment. Lushenska put his sack next to the one the banker had carried, and picked up a small paper bag. Opening it, he reached inside, set the timer on the brick of plastique for three minutes, then slammed the trunk hood shut.

"Now it is time to say good-night. I must contact my people and tell them to proceed. But first I'll walk you to your beautiful car."

He followed Zelnick to the Cadillac and watched as the man got in and sat behind the steering wheel.

The Russian opened the rear door of the American luxury car and dropped the paper sack on the carpeted floor.

"A beautiful car," he told the banker. "I hope you drive carefully. It would be a crime to wreck it."

He returned to his Mercedes, got in, keyed the ignition and raced down the broad street. Through the rearview mirror he could see the huge American car begin to move away from the curb in front of the bank. He suspected Zelnick was in tears. Like most bankers, the man hated giving money away.

The Russian checked his watch. Six seconds to go, and the banker's tears would stop forever.

Five, four, three, two, one.

The buildings near the Cadillac suddenly shuddered as the luxury car exploded. The metal body shattered and turned into metal fragments, showering the area with shards of twisted bits of shrapnel.

Mixed in with the fragments of the car were splinters of human bone and splatters of blood.

The boulevard had become the final resting place of Hans Zelnick. He had finished his business at the bank.

LUSHENSKA TURNED a corner and drove to his office.

The bodies of Kammil Agca and his men were strewed around one of the smaller offices. Their blood had ruined the light-colored wool carpeting. The Russian reached into his pocket and pulled out the fully loaded 9 mm Makarov

PM pistol, then carefully checked the other rooms. Someone had ransacked the files. Fortunately there was nothing that could incriminate him. Lushenska had been discreet about keeping records of clients and field employees.

The Russian knew it hadn't been the police who had raided the suite. There would have been officers on duty waiting for him to return if they had been responsible.

No, this was someone else. He suspected he knew who.

Opening the center drawer of his personal desk, he studied the face of the man who called himself Mike Belasko. From what Lushenska knew of his reputation, the violence and suddenness of the attack fit the descriptions from others of how the American mercenary operated.

Someday the Russian hoped to meet this man—at the muzzle end of a gun. But for now he had too much to do to give it much thought.

He reached under his desk and pulled the rug away to reveal a small safe. Opening it, he reached inside and took out a small leather-covered notebook containing the names of previous clients and unemployed intelligence agents looking for work. There were several passports and identity papers, including a pair of birth certificates a specialist had created for him. He shoved them into his inside pocket.

He searched a nearby closet and found a soft leather bag. Reaching back into the safe, he withdrew thick bound stacks of money that he pushed into the leather carrying case.

Sitting up, he studied the telephone on his desk. There was a temptation to call Brussels and tell Schindler and the American that the assignment was canceled, that the old and the new heads of the arms syndicate were dead.

The Russian decided against it. There was always the chance that someone was eavesdropping on one of the two.

He finally admitted the truth to himself. He didn't much care if either lived or died.

It was time to make a more important call. He lifted the phone and dialed a number.

"Mr. Clemont?"

The voice on the other end growled that it was indeed him, and began to complain about the hour, when Lushenska interrupted.

"This is Viktor Lushenska. I have several jobs for you."

The man's tone changed to one of interest.

"I want you to empty my house of its belongings and put them in storage. You'll find a key to it on my desk at the office, which is where I want you to come first. There are some things here that need to be removed and disposed of."

"How many?"

"I'm not sure. Probably four or five."

"It will be expensive."

"You'll find an envelope filled with money. I am certain there will be more than enough to take care of both my office and my home." He paused. "I'll call you when I return and find out where you've put my possessions."

Opening a side drawer, the Russian took out a manila envelope, then took a thick wad of Swiss francs from his pocket and placed it inside the brown mailing bag.

Clemont would do everything that was necessary. He was a vulgar necessity in Lushenska's business, a disposer of bodies, a specialist who got paid for getting rid of unwanted corpses.

The Russian looked at the watch. It was time to drive to the French border. There was a banker he knew who could launder the funds he was carrying.

As HE GOT into the Mercedes sports car, he thought again about Belasko. Because of his interference, Lushenska was faced with the bother of having to close down his practice temporarily and go into hiding. The Russian didn't have to wonder where the American mercenary was. He was so certain the man was in Brussels to protect his President.

Perhaps the mercenary would kill Rudy Johnson before the man injected the poison into the head of the American government. It would be better if Johnson's death followed the President's.

It was a matter of reputation. He had been hired and paid to kill the American President, and he would fulfill the contract, even though the man who had hired him was dead.

With such a reputation for commitment, he knew he would attract new clients, with difficult assassinations.

Clients who trusted no one would seek his services once they heard that he let nothing stop him from completing the contract—not even the death of the client.

Lushenska thought about the blond woman he had taken to Brussels. If he was lucky, the woman would kill the American mercenary. If she did, she would save him the trouble of hiring someone else to do it. Or having to do it himself.

29

As Bolan came out of the rear door of the safehouse, he looked around. Nobody seemed to be watching. He lifted the hood of the BMW and checked for explosives.

Nothing.

He checked the interior of the trunk. Again it seemed free of explosive devices.

There was one more thing he had to do.

Lowering his back to the ground, the soldier pulled himself under the German-made vehicle and searched for evidence that someone had tampered with the vehicle. The brake lines were sturdy.

The Executioner started to pull himself out from underneath the car when he saw it, a subminiature timing device, hidden behind the gasoline tank and camouflaged to hide its existence. Cautiously he pulled himself to the rear and saw it.

The plastic explosive had been molded and painted to look like a slightly thicker part of the chassis. Only two tiny wires leading from the timing device to an equally tiny detonator could be found.

Bolan stopped and gave the problem he faced some thought.

Glancing at his wristwatch, it was imperative that he start driving to NATO headquarters. Traffic would be heavy, as so many people anxious to see the President of the United States in person would be doing the same thing.

But he knew from past experience that many such devices had become the final resting places for bomb experts trying to remove them. Try to ease one from the surface to which it was attached, and the explosive would immediately detonate. There was no way to be sure if this one was booby-trapped, or if it had a detector that would set off the explosive if the vehicle was moved.

He decided to contact Brognola.

The man on the other end of the telephone line said that Brognola had already left the embassy with the President.

Bolan picked up the miniaturized two-way radio the big Fed had given him and signaled his old friend.

Despite the static, both men could hear each other.

"What's up?"

Bolan hurriedly filled him in.

"Do you need alternate transportation?"

"Yeah. I'm just about ready to rock and roll."

Brognola stopped talking into the microphone. Bolan could hear him giving orders to someone nearby.

"Transportation in fifteen minutes. What about the BMW?"

"I hope the houses nearby are empty."

"They are," Brognola answered. "I had some locals from the embassy check." Then he added an apology. "I don't know how the planter got past them."

"Probably came over the rear fence."

"I'll get the Belgian Intelligence types to start hunting for him. And take care of the BMW."

THE LONG BLACK Lincoln Towncar sporting American flags on both its front fenders waited for Bolan to emerge from the small house. A few minutes later, the big man came out, carrying a number of cases, including the pair he'd brought into the country with him.

The driver of the embassy car jumped out and offered to give him a hand. "Thanks, but just open the door," Bolan said, and climbed into the rear.

Without another word, the driver raced down the small street and turned into one of the wide boulevards that criss-crossed Brussels.

The Executioner checked his watch again. According to the schedule, the President would arrive at NATO in ten minutes.

He leaned forward. "How long to the NATO building?"

"A pair of local police cars will be waiting at the next corner to escort us there." He paused. "Ten minutes at most."

Digging through his canvas carryall, Bolan found the pair of high-powered binoculars he brought and hung them around his neck, then decided to use the time to check his arsenal.

"I SWEAR I PUT IT right next to the gas tank," the young punk whined.

Marin looked skeptical. "So where is the explosion?"

"I don't know."

"Let us go and see this marvelous bomb you claim you attached to the car," the Contractor ordered, slipping a 9 mm Browning Hi-Power pistol into a pocket of his apron.

The pair walked down the street and turned into Rue de Portier.

Leading the way, the nervous bomber pointed to the safe-house. "The car is parked in the rear. I can show you the bomb."

"Show me," Marin ordered.

The two men slipped down the narrow driveway. Pointing to the gas-tank area, the younger man insisted, "It's under there. I swear it is."

The Contractor stared at the street punk, skepticism in his expression.

"I think you're lying," Marin decided, and pulled out the Browning from his pocket.

"No. Don't. You might set the bomb off," the frightened punk cried.

"If there is a bomb," Marin replied, emptying the clip into the chest of his hireling.

Without a word, the young hood stared at Marin, then staggered backward and fell against the car.

The small safehouse shivered, its windows and doors tearing from their frames, as the plastique exploded, tearing the BMW apart and ramming shards of torn metal into the two men. The Contractor was out of business.

BOLAN CHECKED the Beretta 93-R's magazine. It was full, as was the clip for the .44 Magnum Desert Eagle.

He had stripped the Uzi the night before, but checked its magazine. Full.

The Applegate-Fairbairn combat knife felt comfortable mounted on its left forearm sheath.

Opening the latches on the rigid plastic case, the soldier checked that all the parts of the Stoner SR-25 were there. Then he looked at the magazines. They were loaded.

Carefully Bolan assembled the sniper's rifle, snapped a magazine into it and set it on the seat next to him.

The soft plastic bag yielded a 90 mm M-67 recoilless rifle, which was made to be fired from a bipod mount or from a shoulder. Open at both ends, the five-foot-long launcher had a practical range of 2100 meters.

Air cooled and breech loaded, the M-67 was a single-shot weapon. Designed to be used against tanks and armored vehicles, the recoilless rifle could take out most of a company of soldiers.

The Executioner took his time checking the powerful antitank weapon, then looked through the telescopic sight attached to the top to make sure it was operational.

In the bag there were two HEAT rockets wrapped in foam. Both were M-371 A-1 rockets, with a practical firing rate of one to three rounds a minute. Loaded with a HEAT rocket, the unit weighed just over ten pounds.

Knowing he might not have the time later, Bolan loaded one of the rockets into the tubelike weapon and returned the battle-ready unit to its case.

SEVERAL LOCAL POLICEMEN and NATO guards had checked their identification cards several times. The four were tense until the law-enforcement types had finally satisfied themselves that the quartet was really from Television Europe.

Finally alone, Franz asked a question. "How do we get out after we're done here?"

Schindler acknowledged his concern. "There will be a distraction."

Carl stared at her. "What kind of distraction?"

"Somebody will try to grab the hand of the American President. While everybody is grabbing him, I do what I have come to do. Then we get into the Saab and drive away."

"It sounds too simple. We wouldn't get out of the city before the local police found the Saab. And us."

"We won't be in it when they do." The woman smiled. "A car will be waiting for us two miles from here."

Willem looked puzzled. "Who? Why?"

"Remember Josef Kuntzler?"

"That fat pig," Franz snorted. "He turned and got out when things got tough."

"He lives here under the name Josef Kurlyk," Schindler announced.

"I wish I had known sooner," Carl said icily. "He wouldn't be living here or anyplace else."

"That's your problem, Carl. Too impetuous," the woman replied. "Kuntzler owns a large trucking company. I called him.

He'll be waiting to pick us up and smuggle us across the Belgian border."

Franz looked worried. "What if he turns us in?"

"And tell the police who he really is? Not a chance. I called him before I left Geneva."

"And when we cross the border, what do we do?"

"We work our way to Geneva and meet a man who will give us four hundred thousand dollars, U.S."

Willem whistled. "So much?"

"A tiny part of what the people who hired him to find us are paying him," she said.

"And Kuntzler? Under pressure he could still identify us."

Schindler looked at her companions. "Not if we kill him once we cross the border."

She turned and climbed the narrow ladder on the television van that led to the roof platform.

"Time to go to work," she stated.

30

Brognola was waiting for him as the Lincoln pulled to the curb.

"We've checked and checked again. No sign of Johnson or Margaritta Schindler," he whispered when he was close to Bolan.

The Executioner looked around at the growing crowds, studying each sector of the plaza carefully. Some instinct warned him that something was out of place. He couldn't put his finger on exactly what.

"They're here," he replied. "Just make sure the Secret Service people are alert."

Brognola screwed the miniaturized radio receiver into his left ear. "Got yours?"

Bolan pointed to his ear. "Already in."

The big Fed looked at the long black limousine, decorated with American flags on its front fenders, working its way through the growing crowds.

"I've got to go," he apologized. "Stay hard, Striker."

Bolan knew it was Brognola's way of wishing him luck.

The Executioner knew he'd need it if he was going to keep the President alive.

Climbing out of the Lincoln, he saw a pair of local police officers hold up their hands to stop him.

"Let us see your pass," one of them demanded in an officious tone of voice.

The soldier knew he could waste time explaining. Then a voice from behind him snarled an order in French. Bolan could see the suddenly subservient expressions on the faces of the two officers.

Turning, he saw the colonel whom he'd met last night.

The high-ranking military man reached into the back seat of the limousine and pulled out the bag containing the rocket launcher. He carried it up the steps of a nearby observation platform, then climbed down.

"In addition to a handsome rifle, and a rather ugly Uzi, you have two canvas bags inside the car. Do you want them with you?"

"I'll retrieve the bags later. And if you'll hand them to me, I'll carry the weapons."

The colonel reached into the car and brought out the pair of weapons, then stared coldly at the two local police officers as he handed the Stoner and the Uzi to Bolan.

With a final salute, the military man turned and strode away. The Executioner could sense the local cops studying him, wondering who he was to get personal assistance from the colonel.

Ignoring their confused expressions, the Executioner unzipped the bag and took out the rocket launcher, setting it on the floor of the platform. The Stoner SR-25 sniper's rifle was placed next to the antitank weapon and the Uzi SMG next to it.

Bolan didn't feel as if he was overequipped, given the situation and the consequences to the world if he couldn't find and stop the assassins. For the Executioner the ultimate error wasn't having too many weapons, but too few.

Based on previous experience, he knew that no one would even notice the weapons he had spread out. Everyone in the plaza was too busy trying to push for a closer view of the American President to pay any attention to anything else.

THE FORMER CIA deputy director of operations worked his way through the crowds surrounding the presidential limousine.

Wearing the CIA picture identification card he hadn't bothered to turn in when the President forced him to retire, Johnson was able to enlist the help of local policemen in clearing a path.

"I'm supposed to be helping to protect the President," he had explained to a police lieutenant who had been on duty since before the sun rose.

Signaling three officers, the policeman ordered them to help the CIA man reach the American President's vehicle.

As he followed the Belgian policemen, Johnson began to feel some pangs of guilt. He had spent his adult life eliminating the enemies of his country, and now he was about to throw all of that away.

Then he remembered the treatment he had received in the Oval Office, as if he were some low-level clerk. That was the reward he had received for dedicating his life to saving the United States.

Now it was payback time.

As he moved forward, he slipped the ornate ring from his middle finger, then took out the vial he'd concealed in the change pocket of his trousers. Popping the stopper, he dipped the short needle on the outer surface of the ring into the poison in the vial, then waited until he walked over an open sewage drain and dropped the small glass tube and its stopper.

Now he was ready.

He hoped the Russian was right, that no one could detect the existence of the poison in the system after it had done

its deadly work. He had carried no weapons. To do so
would be to admit he was there to attack the President.

He was. But in his own way.

BOLAN LIFTED the binoculars to his eyes and moved them
slowly across the open area in front of the NATO headquarters building. All he could see were hordes of men,
women and children pressing toward the American
limousine.

Six Secret Service agents barred the limousine doors as
the vehicle came to a stop. Bolan could see the micro-Uzi
subguns held in their hands. He knew that each man and
woman had taken a vow to give his or her own life to save
that of the President. Again they were faced with that
possibility.

He swept his binoculars across the plaza, studying the
police observation towers and the camera trucks of the various television organizations. Like the others, the crew
wearing Television Europe jackets was fighting the brisk
breeze, tying down the tripod legs of its cameras.

The soldier turned back to where the limousine had come
to a halt. Through the long lenses, he could see a rear door
open. Somebody inside exchanged words with the Secret
Service guards, then the President stepped out of the vehicle, smiling and waving his hand to the crowds.

Somebody was pushing everyone aside to reach the man
in the White House. Bolan aimed his binoculars at the figure, recognizing Rudy Johnson. For a split second, the soldier thought the President had invited him to join him, but
an examination of the American leader's face indicated he
was surprised.

Waving his guards aside, the President held out his hand.

The Executioner focused on the former CIA man's
hands. Something was wrong with them. He focused tightly

on Johnson's fingers, then saw what it was that had caught his eye.

The ornate ring. Johnson hadn't worn jewelry at the Oval Office, so why now?

Suddenly tense, Bolan spoke into the microphone. "The ring on Johnson's hand may have poison."

He watched as Brognola wrenched the ex-CIA official's hand away and shoved him back. Bolan could see the big Fed shout something to the Secret Service men.

Suddenly Johnson pulled his hand away and tore an edge of it across the back of his other hand. Smiling, the ex-intelligence officer stared at his hand, then closed his eyes and sank to the ground, supported from hitting the walkway by the grip of the Secret Service agents.

From across the plaza, the crowds pressed even closer. The real action was taking place near the main NATO entrance.

Brognola's voice echoed in Bolan's earpiece. "He's dead, Striker. You were right. He was trying to kill the President."

The Executioner lowered the binoculars and took a deep breath of relief. Then a glint of sunlight was reflected into his eyes.

He looked up and saw one of the Television Europe crew lying on his stomach next to the tripod-mounted camera. There was something familiar about the cameraman.

Bolan lifted his binoculars and stared across the plaza. He had seen the face before.

A gust of wind whipped the baseball-style cap from the television cameraman's head.

The man was a woman, a platinum blonde.

He *had* seen her before, in Porto Santos, at another killing of a president.

The woman hadn't seen him. She had turned in the direction of the front of the NATO building, and raised a long rifle to her shoulder, pressing her eye against the scope.

Bolan recognized the weapon as Parker-Hale, an ideal weapon for an assassination.

The soldier started to reach for the Stoner SR-25, then realized there wasn't enough time to accurately aim. The M-67 lay next to the Stoner, fully loaded and ready to fire.

The Executioner raised the tube and rested it on his shoulder. He didn't want to sight the launcher. It would take too much time.

Without missing a beat, Bolan ignited the firing mechanism. Behind him, he could hear the loud gushing sound the escaping gases made.

The noise distracted the blond woman. Turning her head, Bolan saw her stunned look of recognition as she stared at him from the top of the television van. Her eyes never moved from him, even as the HEAT rocket raced at the truck that was her perch.

Bolan could hear male voices shouting in German from behind the truck. "Margaritta, jump!" She never moved. A frozen expression of horror covered her face.

Four bodies and a television truck went airborne as the rocket made contact, while the Executioner flattened his head and body against the floor of the observation platform.

Metal fragments showered the area, several cutting into his face and neck and arms.

He stared at the ground. Miraculously none of the crowd seemed to have sustained serious injuries. Most had already left the immediate area to get a personal glimpse of the visiting American President. The few that had been hurt were still mobile, blood from superficial cuts running down their faces as they raced, screaming, from the area.

The Executioner knew there had been no other way to save the President.

BROGNOLA HELPED Bolan from the observation platform.

"The President would like to say thank-you," the big Fed said, as he walked him to the Lincoln.

"Tell him he's welcome," Bolan replied. "It's time I got out of here."

"I'll tell him," Brognola promised. Then he remembered the weapons on the platform. "And I'll make sure the tools get back to where they belong."

"My bags, too," the Executioner said, stripping off the two handguns and combat knife and dropping them into one of his canvas carryalls.

"No problem," Brognola answered as he took the heavy bags from the Executioner.

Getting into the embassy vehicle, Bolan instructed the driver to take him to the airport, then leaned his head back against the cushioned seat.

This battle had been won, but the war raged on.

As long as people like Lushenska were alive, there would always be new front lines.

As the Lincoln raced along the boulevards to the airport, the Executioner closed his eyes and concentrated on a word that kept popping into his head.

Peace.

In the world. And inside himself.

Would it ever come?

Under Attack!

STONY MAN™ 34

REPRISAL

In a brilliant conspiracy to restore the glory days of the CIA, a rogue agent has masterminded a plot to take out Company competition. His stolen clipper chip has effectively shut down the Farm's communications network and made sitting ducks of the field teams. With Phoenix Force ambushed and trapped in the Colombian jungle, and a cartel wet team moving in on Able Team stateside, it's up to Mack Bolan and the Stony experts to bring off the impossible.

Available in April 1998 at your favorite retail outlet.

Where there's smoke...

THE Destroyer™

#111 Prophet of Doom

Created by
WARREN MURPHY
and RICHARD SAPIR

Everyone with a spare million is lining up at the gates of Ranch Ragnarok, home to Esther Clear Seer's Church of the Absolute and Incontrovertible Truth. Here an evil yellow smoke shrouds an ancient oracle that offers glimpses into the future. But when young virgins start disappearing, CURE smells something more than a scam—and Remo is slated to become a sacrificial vessel....

Look for it in April 1998 wherever Gold Eagle books are sold.

James Axler

OUTLANDERS™

PARALLAX RED

Kane and his colleagues stumble upon an ancient colony on Mars that housed a group of genetically altered humans, retained by the Archons to do their bidding. After making the mat-trans jump to Mars, the group finds itself faced with two challenges: a doomsday device that could destroy Earth, and a race of Transhumans desperate to steal human genetic material to make moving to Earth possible.

In the Outlands, the future is an eternity of hell....

GOLD EAGLE®

GOUT5

Don't miss out on the action in these titles featuring THE EXECUTIONER®, STONY MAN™ and SUPERBOLAN®!

The American Trilogy

#64222	PATRIOT GAMBIT	$3.75 U.S.	☐
		$4.25 CAN.	☐
#64223	HOUR OF CONFLICT	$3.75 U.S.	☐
		$4.25 CAN.	☐
#64224	CALL TO ARMS	$3.75 U.S.	☐
		$4.25 CAN.	☐

Stony Man™

#61910	FLASHBACK	$5.50 U.S.	☐
		$6.50 CAN.	☐
#61911	ASIAN STORM	$5.50 U.S.	☐
		$6.50 CAN.	☐
#61912	BLOOD STAR	$5.50 U.S.	☐
		$6.50 CAN.	☐

SuperBolan®

#61452	DAY OF THE VULTURE	$5.50 U.S.	☐
		$6.50 CAN.	☐
#61453	FLAMES OF WRATH	$5.50 U.S.	☐
		$6.50 CAN.	☐
#61454	HIGH AGGRESSION	$5.50 U.S.	☐
		$6.50 CAN.	☐

(limited quantities available on certain titles)

TOTAL AMOUNT	$
POSTAGE & HANDLING	$
($1.00 for one book, 50¢ for each additional)	
APPLICABLE TAXES*	$ _____
TOTAL PAYABLE	$ _____
(check or money order—please do not send cash)	

To order, complete this form and send it, along with a check or money order for the total above, payable to Gold Eagle Books, to: **In the U.S.**: 3010 Walden Avenue, P.O. Box 9077, Buffalo, NY 14269-9077; **In Canada**: P.O. Box 636, Fort Erie, Ontario, L2A 5X3.

Name: _____

Address: _____ City: _____

State/Prov.: _____ Zip/Postal Code: _____

*New York residents remit applicable sales taxes.
  Canadian residents remit applicable GST and provincial taxes.

GEBACK19

**A violent struggle for survival
in a post-holocaust world**

JAMES AXLER

DEATH LANDS ®

Freedom Lost

Following up rumors of trouble on his old home ground, Ryan and his band seek shelter inside the walls of what was once the largest shopping mall in the Carolinas. The baron of the fortress gives them no choice but to join his security detail. As outside invaders step up their raids on the mall, Ryan must battle both sides for a chance to save their lives.